SAM ADKINS

ANTECEDENT

REBORN

BOOK 2

D1714424

To Sam

Susan Stumpf

Susan Stumpf

Editing by Masque of the Red Pen

Photography by Rachel Cole

Interior and Cover Design by

Alpha Queens Book Obsession

For Brian...
my favorite blue-haired sidekick.

Susan Stumpf

ONE

Finding an Antecedent was not an easy task. It had taken me three months. I'd become a seed hunter hunter. I went to all the antique auctions in the area looking for seed hunters. I never saw the one that had come to my house. I was glad, but it made them hard to find. I spotted a suspicious looking set of men a couple of times but lost them when I tried to follow them after the auctions. One evening I was sitting in my car after an auction, and I saw two men grab a guy and shove him in their trunk.

"Bingo!" I said aloud and started my car. I followed them for hours. I almost lost them once we got into the heavy traffic of Charlotte. Had it been rush hour I would have lost them for sure. Once the interstate, I backed off a bit hoping they wouldn't notice me. It was after midnight, and there weren't many cars on the side streets.

We drove on the side roads for awhile until the car pulled up to a large house with a gate at the bottom of a long driveway. I pulled over just down the street but still within sight and watched. The car sat there for a moment then the gate opened then shut quickly after they went through. Well, this was it. I guess I was just going to drive over there and see what happens. I didn't drive all this way for nothing. I took a deep breath then drove up to the gate. There was a metal box on a pole about window level, and it had a button and a speaker. I rolled my window down and pressed the button, the buzzing of the box startled me. A voice came back a moment later.

"Yeah, what do you want?" a man sounding bored asked.

"Um, I'm here to see your boss." I wasn't sure what to say really.

"Do you have an appointment?" the voice asked.

"No, but…"

"Then buzz off," he interrupted.

It was going to take more than that to stop me. I pressed the button again.

"I thought I told you to buzz off," the voice said.

"Look, I know an Antecedent lives here, and I want to see him."

"I don't know what you're talking about, now go away."

I pressed the button five more times.

"What the hell is your problem, lady?"

"I know you know what I'm talking about. I just followed two seed hunters here who had stuffed an unchanged seed in their trunk. I know he was brought here to be forced to become an Antecedent, and I know that you're probably an Ectype just doing your job. All I want to do is talk to your boss for one minute, please."

There was silence, and I thought the guy was just going to ignore me, but just when I was about to press the button again he said, "Alright, come on in." A buzzer sounded, and the gate opened. Okay, that wasn't so hard.

I drove up the driveway that made a large circle in front of the house. The house was pretty big, like the ones you'd see in

Beverly Hills. I couldn't make out many details of it because there were no outside lights at all. The only light was coming from a sliver of the moon and my headlights. The car I followed here was sitting in front of the house with the trunk open, but no one was around. I was almost afraid to shut my car off and step out into the darkness. Well, here goes nothing, I told myself. I got out of the car and walked up to the door. I knocked and waited just a moment for it to open. Light spilled out as the door opened, and I wasn't sure what to expect. A very handsome man opened the door. He could have been a Stetson model with his square jaw and perfectly combed back hair. He was wearing dark jeans, cowboy boots, and a dark blue sports coat. Well helloooo, Mr. Doorman.

"Alright, little Miss persistent," another man said as I stepped inside. "What can we do for you this evening?"

I looked to my left and the man speaking was sitting in an office chair. He had thinning light brown hair cut close and facial hair that reminded me of a movie villain. He was seated at a long curved desk. It was a security station. I could see a couple dozen monitors showing different scenes, inside and outside the house.

"I um, I'd like to speak with your boss for a moment if I could please," I asked timidly.

I was known for being an intrepid girl but being in this house, one that was probably filled to brim with vampires, I didn't feel brave at all. At any given moment any one of them could kill me in an instant for no reason at all. The movie villain motioned his head sideways, and a third guy I hadn't seen walked off quickly.

"Wait here please," Dreamy door hunk told me. I stood there looking around. This place was impressive. The floors were ivory with black diamonds and small squares that looked like mother of pearl, very high ceilings; there was a gigantic crystal chandelier. In front of us was an ornate staircase that split in two different directions at the top. It reminded me of the staircase in Gone with the Wind, red carpet and all. There was a black statue of a woman who looked like a Greek goddess, and she was holding a glowing ball in her hands. That had to be the coolest lamp I'd ever seen. We needed to get a couple of those in the antique shop. Oh wow, I was starting to sound like Bo. I think antiques were starting to grow on me.

The scrawny little guy came back and motioned for me to follow him. "Well, it's your lucky night," movie villain guy said.

I followed the little guy down a hallway to the right. We walked past the longest painting I'd ever seen. It was probably twelve feet long. It was men on horseback, like a Revolutionary War scene. We continued down the hallway past tons of hideous pictures in gaudy gold frames, then finally we stopped at a door. The little guy walked through, held it open for me then left shutting it behind him. I suddenly felt a chill of impending doom. I walked into what I guessed was a game room. The walls were blood red and looked fuzzy; it was an eyesore. There were two large pool tables with gold yarn sacks for pockets and a card table where half a dozen men were sitting playing poker.

I walked over and stood there for a minute, and no one spoke to me or even looked at me, so I cleared my throat. One older looking man held his finger up to me then threw a stack of chips in the middle of the table. The rest of the men followed in placing their bets and then revealed their cards. The rest of the men groaned while one raked all the chips in the pot to himself and started stacking them in front of him.

"So," the older man spoke, "I hear you know all about vampires, little one. What is it exactly that you want?"

He had a bit of an accent, but I couldn't place it. I guessed that this man was the Antecedent. He was much older than I thought he'd be. Wu said most Ants were turned between the ages of twenty and thirty. This guy had to be around fifty. He had black hair that was slicked back and grayed around his temples. His eyes were red, not his pupils like in the movies, but bloodshot. He looked old and tired. He was wearing a red shirt that I could only describe as an ugly woman's blouse.

"I'd like to speak with you for just a moment in private if I could please," I replied.

"The only way we will have a word in private is if you plan on making that private time worth my while." He looked up from his newly dealt cards to look me up and down.

No way Dracula, I thought to myself. "I just wanted to ask you something."

He sighed, disinterested like he was bored with our conversation already.

"Let me guess, little one, you want me to turn you. Your little heart has been broken, and you don't want to be mortal any longer. Am I correct?"

Okay, so I guess he's heard this all before.

"So will you or won't you?" I got right to the point.

"What's in it for me?" he asked. "Shall we go have that private time?"

"Ew! No!" I said, not caring if I offended him.

"Franco," he said and motioned with two fingers, and a man who had been standing in the corner walked over.

"Kill her. Take her upstairs for someone to eat," he said flatly.

"Wait, NO!" I protested.

The Antecedent motioned for Franco to take me away, and the guy grabbed my arm. I pulled and jerked and fought to get away, but this guy was a vamp and way too strong for me to escape his grasp.

Franco pulled me along out the door. I fought him the whole way. If they were going to kill me, it wasn't going to be an easy task. He dragged me flailing down the hallway. He had a grip on the sleeve of my sweater, and I was able to pull my arm through it and back out of my sweater. I tried to run, but I only made it two steps before he grabbed me again. He dragged me up a set of stairs. I fought so hard we both stumbled on the stairs. We passed another man who spoke.

"Hey you need a hand, Franco?" the man laughed.

"Sure, this one's a pistol," he answered.

"Where we taking her?"

"Arlo said to take her upstairs, feed her to one of the guys."

"No, nooo!" I protested as I squirmed even harder. They paid no attention to me at all, just kept talking about me like I wasn't even there.

"Seems a shame," the new guy said. "She's kind of hot. I wonder if she's this fiery in the bedroom."

With that, I kicked his leg as hard as I could but he just laughed, and they continued to drag me down another hallway. Now I wished I hadn't backed out of my sweater; they were pulling me along in nothing but my bra and Capri tights. I'd lost my slippers on the stairs.

We came to a door, and Franco knocked a couple times then opened it. It was a large, fancy bedroom, but I didn't see anyone inside.

"Hey, buddy, we brought you a snack," the other one said.

They pushed me into the room. I felt something hit the back of my head, and everything went black.

I awoke lying in a bed. I clearly hadn't thought this whole thing out. I thought either they would say yes and I'd be made a vampire, or they would say no and send me away. I hadn't really considered the possibility of being eaten or murdered. I don't guess I'd be living with that mistake very long. I was in a large bedroom divided into a sleeping area and a sitting area by a small wall. The head of the bed was up against the partition. I got up and walked around the other side. There was a couch, a desk, and a TV mounted to the other side of the partition. There was a large window. I walked over to it. I couldn't tell if it was dark outside or if the windows were tinted. Tinted windows would make sense in a house full of vampires. The window wasn't the kind that opened. I didn't know how I was going to get out of here. Any minute now, somebody was going to walk in, and I was going to become their bedtime snack.

I walked back to the other side of the room. There was no one in this room with me, but somebody had to have put me on the bed. Then someone came walking out of what I think was the bathroom.

"Well, you're finally awake." I knew that voice. I stood there stunned. It was Wu.

"I'm glad you are. You're far too pretty to eat, sweetheart. I've got far greater plans for you."

Did he not recognize me? Is this why he hadn't come home? Did he not know who he was? Did he have amnesia or something? He looked at me smiling, fangs showing behind his lips.

"I guess you don't need this now." He was holding a wet washcloth. He took a step toward me, and I took a step backward.

"Don't fight it, sweetheart; there's nowhere to run." He winked at me. That wink! Did he know who I was, who he was? He grabbed me. Oh no! Of all the ways I would ever die, I never thought it would be at the hands of Wu not knowing who I was. He wrapped his arms around me and whispered in my ear.

"Just go with it, Em. I'm going to try and save your life the only way I know how."

"Oh, Wu," I whispered back. I breathed a huge sigh of relief. He kissed me long and hard. I didn't feel that way about Wu, but I kissed him back mainly because I was so glad he was alive and he wasn't going to kill me.

"We're being watched," he whispered again.

He unhooked my bra and took it off, and I backed away from him, covering myself. What was he doing? If we were being watched, I definitely didn't want to get naked.

"Come on now don't be shy, sweetheart," he said loudly. "If you prefer I could just drain you of blood and be done with you. It's your choice really."

I didn't completely understand, but I guess my choices were: have sex with Wu or die.

"Okay," I said. Stepping toward him, I put my hands on his bare chest. He was wearing some black lounge pants. He looked pretty much the same as he always did. His skin had always been a warm suntanned color synonymous with his oriental descent but wasn't now. He looked a little pasty; the paleness didn't suit him.

"Good girl." He winked at me again.

He finished undressing me then took off his pants also. We walked over to the bed. I'd never gotten myself into a predicament quite like this before...have sex or die! At least it was Wu; he's someone I cared for and trusted. It's not like he was a stranger. The guys that brought me up here said they were going to feed me to one of the guys upstairs so there must be more vampires, more bedrooms. I wonder what would've happened if they would have taken me to a different room. I'd probably be dead right now, drained of all my blood and laying on the floor.

Wu positioned his body on top of me and kissed me again. Here we go. I couldn't believe I was about to have sex with Wu. He pretended to kiss my neck but whispered, "Okay, Em, some of this I can fake, but I really am going to have to bite you, okay? I'm so sorry."

I turned my head to expose more of my neck to him. He bit me but didn't drink near as long as Bo ever did. He kept his head there creating the façade that he was drinking longer.

I wasn't sure what he meant by faking some of it until I realized we weren't actually going to have sex. He was just pretending. I wasn't even sure he had taken enough blood from me to accomplish the task. Vampires needed blood to increase their circulation. He didn't really drink, he just bit me and pretended to drink. He went through the motions and made it look believable. I tried to be a good actress and make a few noises, but it was horribly embarrassing. Being completely naked in front of Wu, him laying on top of me naked, and knowing someone somewhere was watching what we were doing. I was thankful it didn't last long. Wu laid down next to me, and there was nothing but silence for awhile, then he moved his head onto my pillow and whispered, "What the hell are you doing here, Em?"

"I hunted down the Ant so I could ask him to turn me," I answered.

"What? Why?"

"I'm tired of having feelings. I don't want to be hurt anymore. I want to be cold and not care. I want to be a vampire."

"And Bo didn't try to talk you out of this?" he asked.

"Bo's gone, Wu, he left."

"Left where?"

"He went back to Lithuania, said he'd be back in fifty years or so. Then Esther died, and it has just been horrible since you left."

"Esther died, how?"

"It was after Bo left, she died in her bed. I think it just broke her heart that he left. He didn't even come back for her funeral."

"What about Umpa, is he okay?" he asked.

"Yes, he's fine. He's been working the store, and I've been helping. I go over to your house sometimes to check on him and chat so he doesn't get too lonely."

"Thanks, Em." He smiled and kissed me on the forehead.

We lay there just a little while longer then Wu stood up and started getting dressed.

"Where are you going?" I asked.

"I'm still hungry," he said.

That made sense; he hadn't taken much blood from me at all.

"Do you want something?" he asked.

"Yes please anything!" I skipped dinner, and now it was close to morning, so I was starving.

"Stay here," he said. "Do not leave this room for anything! Do you understand?"

I nodded.

I put my clothes back on while he was gone...well, what clothes I had. Who knows where my sweater was. They probably threw it away since I was supposed to be dead right now. All I had were tights and my under things, so I climbed back under the covers.

He wasn't gone long. He must have found something or someone to eat in the house. He didn't have to go out and hunt. He also came back with half a container of Pringles and an apple for me. I asked to borrow one of his shirts, and we sat on the couch and talked while I ate. I was under the impression that he was being held captive here. I guess if you're going to be held prisoner, a mansion in a big cushy room was the place to be. After we'd sat there talking for awhile, I heard a very strange noise. It was a sound playing over like a loud speaker.

"Is that…is that a rooster crowing?" I looked at him confused.

"Yes, it's an alarm. It's almost morning."

He got up and released the pull back on the thick, heavy curtains that hung over the already blacked out window. I guess vampires can never be too careful.

"Let's go to bed," he said, and we walked arm in arm back across the room. I was so happy to see that there was an actual toilet in the bathroom even though I was in a vampire house. I'd asked Bo about that one day months back. He told me that vampires didn't need toilets. He said that the blood a vampire consumes is completely used up; there was no waste like with human food. Vampires' bodies used every bit of blood they consumed, so there was no need for them, it was just wasted space. I crawled into bed with Wu and just before he passed out cold the way vampires do, he kissed me on the forehead.

"Get some sleep, Em," he whispered. "Tomorrow, I'm going to save your life."

Antecedent: Reborn

I slept soundly despite being in a strange place. I'd been so scared tonight and was so relieved to find Wu. I slept very closely to him but tried to remind myself that he wasn't the same Wu. He was a vampire now. I awoke in the afternoon but knew Wu wouldn't wake up till after sunset, some five hours from now. I woke up hungry, but I wasn't going to leave this room for anything. I didn't think Wu was acting for the camera when he warned me not to leave. There was nothing stopping someone from killing me on the spot if I walked out that door. I showered, then sat on Wu's small couch and watched TV until sunset. Hopefully, soon I would find out how exactly he planned to save my life.

It was the next day, well, the next vampire day. The day was night and the night was day. Although it was eight p.m., Wu told me good morning when he got up. Sometimes keeping up with both worlds was maddening. Wu showered and dressed and asked if I was ready to go downstairs.

"Sure," I said hesitantly.

He kissed me on the cheek and whispered to me, "Just keep quiet and go along with everything I say."

As we left the room Wu grabbed my hand and interlaced his fingers with mine. We walked down the hallway I'd been dragged down yesterday and down the stairs. We walked into a few rooms only to walk right back out again. We found Arlo in what I guessed was some sort of sitting room or parlor. It had a lot of furniture but nothing else.

The room was hideous, with rectangular burgundy wooden panels lining the walls. I don't know who they got to decorate this place, but I hoped they ate them so they couldn't do this to any other houses. What was it with vampires and bad décor? There was a lot of clunky antique looking furniture, and none of it matched any other piece. The room was an eyesore. Although, there was one of those circular high back chairs with a lamp coming up the middle of it, and I had a strong urge to sit in it and see how they got the lamp up through it. Focus, Em, focus…room full of vampires. Get your head in the game.

"Arlo, I wish to speak with you about this woman," Wu said as we approached the creepy old man from yesterday.

"Playing with your food, brother Wu?" Arlo asked.

Wu squeezed my hand in reassurance and pulled me a little closer to his side.

"This woman is no food, nor will she be. She is now carrying my child, and I wish to have her released from this house," Wu spoke confidently.

Susan Stumpf

Arlo raised one eyebrow and looked at us skeptically.

"Is she now?"

Arlo then spoke to the scrawny guy who had led me to the game room last night. "Fetch me Dante."

The little guy returned in just a few seconds with the guy who'd been sitting at the security station last night.

"You were on watch last night, were you not?" Arlo asked him.

"Yes," he answered.

"And did you see anything interesting going on in brother Wu's room?"

"Oh yeah, they did it," he said with a smug smile on his face. It turned my stomach to think that this guy was watching us.

"She was quite willing in fact," he said and ran the backs of his fingers down my arm. I jerked away, and Wu stepped over and grabbed him by the throat.

"She's mine, Ectype!" Wu growled at him. It was the only time I'd ever seen Wu look scary.

"Yes, yes, Dante, you know the rules." Wu released the man as Arlo spoke. "If brother Wu has claimed her, you must respect his wishes."

"Well then, tell me girl, what is your name?" Arlo asked.

"Her name is Emina," Wu answered for me. Oh, why did he give my whole name? Great, a house full of nasty vampires calling me by my whole name.

"Well, Emina, if Wu has indeed taken a liking to you then feel free to stay here as long as you like."

Arlo spoke like he knew what we were up to, like he didn't believe us. He spoke to Wu with a fake affection that was obvious to pick up on. They were definitely frienemies.

"She doesn't want to stay here, she wants to leave," Wu said. "As the mother of my child, I don't want her to be held here against her will. I can arrange for my kin to take her in and care for her and the child."

"Well this is all well and good, brother, but how do you know that you have in fact impregnated her? You only had her once. Tell me my dear, when did you last bleed?"

Ah…was he talking to me, seriously?

"None of your business, geez," I answered. I wasn't going to talk about my period in front of all these vampire men.

"Answer the question, Em," Wu said squeezing my hand.

"I don't know, like two or three weeks ago I guess. I don't have my calendar."

"Well that is ideal timing," Arlo said. "But just once isn't enough to be sure. Let's have her stay the week, and you can continue to bed her. Then if she still wishes to leave, we will discuss it then. Agreed?"

"Agreed," Wu said.

We turned around and walked out of the room, and quietly talked once we were clear of people.

"You're safe now," Wu said.

"I don't understand, why am I safe now?"

"If they believe you are carrying a seed, no one can touch you. Seeds are precious commodities. They ensure the future of vampires. No one can harm you, but now the problem will be getting you out of the house. I think I have enough power that if I insist, it is possible."

"You have power here? I thought you were a prisoner?" I whispered.

"Technically I have almost as much power as Arlo. He and I are both Antecedents now. I'm not a prisoner here, but Arlo is very much against me leaving. If I forced the issue I could leave, but I want to find out why he is so adamant about me staying here."

"So all the vampires here aren't Antecedents?"

"No, there's Arlo and I and one other right now. I've also seen two other men come as seeds and leave as Antecedents since I've been here."

"And Arlo just let them leave?"

"Yes, but when I asked to leave he went on and on about how Antecedents need to be careful and protected. Every time, he'd suggest I stay a bit longer. Now I want to know why."

"Some seed hunters brought a man in last night. I followed them here."

"Really?" he asked, interested. "I'll go and see what I can find out about him. You should be fine now. If anybody gives you any trouble at all, tell them you belong to me and to take it up with Arlo."

"Okay," I answered tensely. "Where can I find something to eat? I'm starving."

Wu pointed me in the direction of the kitchen then went off to find out what he could about the new arrival. I didn't want him to leave me alone. What if somebody tried to kill me before I could explain that I belonged to Wu? I decided I would find something to eat then go back to Wu's room and stay…if I could find my way back, that is. We'd taken so many twists and turns I wasn't sure which way to go. This place was huge.

I walked into the swinging door of the kitchen. It was a strange little room, forming a perfect circle. Cabinets and appliances lined the walls, and there was a small circular table with four chairs in the middle. The room looked like a giant donut, and that thought only made me hungrier. A woman was rummaging through one of the cabinets. This was the first girl I'd seen; the house was full of men. I didn't know if she was human or vampire. I'd never seen a female vampire before. I was getting the feeling they were rare.

"Ah, did somebody eat my Pringles?" she said annoyed.

"Oh yeah, that was me. Sorry," I said.

She turned around quickly and glared at me. I'd only seen the back of her, but now that she'd turned around I could see that she was pregnant. She looked to be maybe four months along. She had dark, stringy shoulder length hair and a turned up nose. Have you ever looked at somebody and just knew you wouldn't get along with them? That was this girl. Okay, so Pringles and pregnant, definitely human! She slammed the cabinet door shut.

"…and just who are you?" she asked.

"Hi, I'm Em." I tried to smile, but I was obviously on this girl's bad side now that I'd eaten her chips. Taking a pregnant lady's food is dangerous.

"Well just so you know, I'm Arlo's emissary so don't ever touch my stuff!" she said and walked out another door opposite of the one I'd walked in.

"Pay no attention to Jackie," someone said in a deep Southern accent. "She's got an over inflated sense of self-worth."

I turned to see a girl sitting on the counter behind the door I'd just walked through. She was in a football jersey and really short shorts. She looked like a model from a men's magazine. She was beautiful. Her hair hung off her head in perfect red wisps.

"Emissary my derriere," she continued, "that's just a fancy word for whore." But she pronounced it ho-wah. I loved this girl's accent! I could listen to her speak all day. She jumped down off the counter.

"Hi there, I'm René. Welcome to the bordello of blood," she laughed.

"Hi," I said.

"You hungry, sugah?" she asked.

"Starving," I answered.

She opened the fridge and compiled the makings of two sandwiches.

"Where are you from?" I asked curious about the source of her southern accent.

"I was born and raised in Shreveport, Louisiana. I moved to Tennessee to pursue my singing career. As you can see, I didn't get very far. I've been here for two years now."

I wondered how old she was. She looked fairly young, nineteen or twenty was my guess, but I didn't ask. I didn't want to seem too nosey, although she seemed to be a very open kind of person.

"I've been here for twenty-four hours," I said as I sat in a chair at the small round table in the center of the room.

"Who brought you here?" she asked.

"Umm...nobody, I came here myself."

She looked at me confused. I explained to her in sparse detail how I'd come here hoping to be turned but was denied and thrown into Wu's room as a snack, but how lucky I was that he took a liking to me.

"I was brought here by none other than Bobby; I would've followed that man anywhere." She said it like I should know who she was talking about. I shook my head.

"Oh you'd know him if you saw him, he may have greeted you at the door."

"Ohhh," I said, "the one who looks like a young Sean Connery?"

"Yes ma'am, that'd be him."

"Can't say that I blame you there," I smiled, and she laughed.

She set a plate with a sandwich down in front of me and sat down next to me. She propped her feet up on the chair on the other side.

"Stick with me, sugah, I'll show ya the ropes 'round here," she said taking a bite.

We talked while we ate, and when we were done, René washed our plates and put them away.

"Hey you wanna go veg in the TV room?" she asked me.

"Sure," I answered.

I felt remotely safe with René. She'd been here for a couple of years now, so I didn't think anybody would bother me if I was with her. Besides, hanging out with her sounded better than hiding out in Wu's room all night. I followed her through twists and turns. I was totally lost. There were hallways everywhere.

"How did you ever find your way around this place?" I asked.

"It took some time," she laughed. "Basically there are six hallways down here and four staircases. I tell the hallways apart by the painting at the beginning: there's the Viking hallway, hunter hallway, and the two war hallways. There are two in the east wing, and two in the west wing; each pair is adjoined by another hallway on the ends. Upstairs, the apocalypse is to your left and boats to your right. You just have to learn which paintings lead to what."

"We just walked down the Revolutionary War hallway and up the secondary staircase. We are now at the end of the boat hallway; your room is also down this way," she explained.

We walked through an archway with double doors into a cozy room with the biggest TV I'd ever seen. It was surrounded by comfortable looking furniture. She plopped down on the couch, and I sat beside her. She flipped through the channels and stopped on one of those forensic crime shows. She was one of those people who talked all the way through a TV show so you missed what was going on, but I didn't mind. I was happy to spend time with someone who didn't want to kill me.

We were most of the way through the show when that small guy from last night walked into the room. "Hey, René," he said.

"Hey, Mickey," she said then clapped her hands..."Hey, Mickey, you're so fine, you're so fine you blow my mind, hey Mickey!" She clapped again. Wow, seriously? Was this girl my long lost twin or what?

"Em, have you met Mickey?" she asked.

"Yes, I believe he led me to my impending doom last night," I said semi-jokingly.

"Ah Mickey's a sweetheart," she said getting up and putting her arm around him. He smiled, exposing his fangs, and she kissed him on the cheek. If it were possible for a vampire to blush, I believe he would have.

"Franco wants you," Mickey said to her.

"Egh," she sighed, "alright."

She turned back to me. "Tell me later who killed that guy's brother and why," she said referring to the show we'd been watching. Then they both turned and walked toward the door. René smacked him on the butt as she walked faster past him. I laughed. She was so spirited and vivacious, what was she doing in such a dark, creepy place like this?

I watched the rest of the show so I could let René know what happened later. I sat there the rest of the day, still a little scared to walk around by myself. I did retrace our steps back to the kitchen later to grab something to eat. I didn't know what belonged to Jackie and what was free reign, so I grabbed a couple pieces of fruit from the basket in the middle of the table and went back upstairs to the TV room. This is where Wu found me. He didn't say anything; he just reached out his hand to me. I grabbed it and stood up. He twirled me around once like we were dancing and pulled me in front of him with his arm around me.

"It's time for act two, Em, I'm sorry," he whispered in my ear.

Were there cameras in here, too? Were there cameras everywhere?

We went back to his room which was right down the hall like René said it was. We put on our façade of having sex, and I went to sleep in his arms. The rooster crowing alarm woke me up, and I couldn't go back to sleep. I probably only slept for maybe two hours. I lay there thinking about Wu. He didn't seem much different than before he was changed. He still seemed so loving. We didn't even have real sex, just pretend sex and here Wu was holding me. Bo never did that, even after real sex. Maybe the coldness wasn't a vampire thing, but a Bo thing. Wu was always a kind and loving person, and he still seemed kind and loving now. Perhaps Bo wasn't a warm and caring human. Therefore he wasn't a warm and caring vampire. Maybe he wasn't even capable of love as a human; I guess some people are just that way. A tear rolled down my cheek. Why is it the ones you want to love you the most are the ones who don't? Okay, I had to get up. I wasn't going to lay here and think about Bo.

I thought about watching TV, but I'd done that all day and wasn't interested. I could probably explore the house fairly safely since the sun was up now, all the vampires would be sleeping. I got dressed in the only clothes I had: my leggings and the t-shirt I borrowed from Wu. I slipped out the door and left it cracked. I hoped Wu wouldn't mind because I wasn't completely sure which door was ours in the hallway full of similar looking ones. Then I remembered what René said about using the pictures and paintings as landmarks. Outside our room was a picture of a ship on a stormy sea. Okay, I'd remember that just in case. I tried to remember what René said about the hallways. I walked to the end and looked at the large picture at the beginning of the hallway. A dozen ships in a harbor. Okay… that's easy enough; I just have to remember to follow the boats home.

I walked down the split of the main staircase and back up the other side to the other hallway and examined that painting. It was horrifying. It was hundreds of people being tortured and dragged off by little devil looking beings. This is what René called the apocalypse hallway. I walked down it but saw nothing but closed doors. I wasn't about to open any of them, not knowing what was behind them. Toward the end of that hallway were two men standing in front of a big metal cage of a wall, and inside the cage was a vault door. This must be Arlo's room. The men, obviously human, went rigid at my approach. I held up my hands to show them I wasn't a threat and turned around and went back the way I came.

I walked down the Gone with the Wind staircase. René said there were three other sets of stairs. We'd used another one going from the kitchen to the TV room, but I had no idea where the other two were. I picked a hallway and examined the first hanging picture. It was a battle, men carrying a rebel flag. The Civil War hallway. Down this hallway, I found a large library. I wasn't much of a reader, but I could appreciate its beauty. It was the kind you saw in movies with the ladder that slides on rails all the way around. I was so tempted to run and jump on and see how far I could slide around the shelves, but I was afraid I'd make too much noise. There wasn't much else down this hallway: a piano lounge and an office.

I came to an intersection and was a little nervous about getting lost. René said there were only six hallways downstairs. To the right and down the hall a bit was a staircase. I assumed from where I was that it led upstairs right around Arlo's room, and I didn't want to be anywhere near there, so I went left. This hallway was much shorter than the one I'd just been down. All that was really down here was a utility room and a laundry room. Good to know, seeing how I'd been wearing the same underwear for almost three days now. This hallway ended and turned left into another long hallway. Down this one amongst a few closed doors, there was a ballroom and the sitting room Wu and I had spoken with Arlo in.

I was back in the foyer... okay, this wasn't too complicated. I'd gone down the back hallway and come out the front. I turned and looked at the painting at the end of this hallway and committed it to memory, Vikings. I stood there making a mental note: The Civil War leads to the library and laundry room, Vikings lead to the sitting room and ballroom, and how befitting it was that the apocalypse led to Arlo. The guys at the security station looked at me just standing there giving me their most intimidating glare. They were obviously human; I'd battled vampires, so I wasn't the slightest bit intimidated by these two men. I crossed the foyer and planned on doing the same thing on this side.

I went down the back, Revolutionary War hallway; this was the one I'd walked down when I first got here. So I knew the game room was down here. The kitchen was just off the foyer on this side also. I found an arcade; I would definitely have to remember that, and an exercise room and another set of stairs, the ones I'd taken up to the TV room yesterday. I also found another laundry room; there was one for each wing. The layout was the same as the other side. I'd come full circle and was back in the foyer again. I examined the painting at the end. It was men in red coats wearing those hideous Capri pants and ugly shoes on horseback with a bunch of hounds, English hunters. Okay, Revolutionary War leads to the game room and arcade, English hunters leads to exercise room and laundry room. So that's six hallways but only three staircases. There must be either an attic or basement.

I looked around. I thought I'd covered the whole place, but then I noticed that there was a cubby hole behind the grand staircase. I walked over to get a closer look. Was I allowed back here? I looked across the foyer to the guys at the security station.

They weren't paying any attention to me now; I guess they had gotten used to me walking around everywhere. They were looking at the monitors and talking. There was a storage room back here and a door. Dare I open it? Sure, why not. I opened the door to find a staircase leading down. I cautiously walked down the stairs and got a chill. I didn't know if it was the creepy feeling I was getting or the sting of the cold concrete against my bare feet.

I was in a small hallway that looked like a jail or torture chamber or something. There were two doors on each side, the kind that had barred windows at the top. I looked into the windows as I tiptoed down the hallway. Nothing in the first two, nothing in the last one to the left. I thought for a second they were all empty, but in the last one, there was a man laying naked on the floor curled up into the fetal position. I got another chill; was he dead? I kept walking; there were large doors to the right and to the left. I chose the one to the right. It was a heavy metal door, so it creaked when I opened it.

I saw flashing lights, like a strobe coming from more cell doors. I looked through the barred window and saw a man on the floor. He was also naked, but this man wasn't laying there lifeless like the other; he was moaning and writhing, and his skin looked burned.

"Hey," a man yelled at me, scaring me half to death as he and another man came running up to me.

"What are you doing down here?"

Oh, no. I didn't know how I was going to get out of this one.

Okay Em, I told myself, show time. Lay it on thick.

"Oh goodness gracious," I said, playfully smacking the man on the chest.

"You scared me half to death," I smiled at him.

"What are you doing down here?" he asked a little less forcefully. This guy was huge. He was muscular and bald. He looked like one of those pro wrestlers.

"Oh, honey. I am SO lost. Can you help me please?" I asked, batting my eyelashes at him. "I'm new here, and I have gotten myself so turned around."

Someone said something over a radio that I didn't hear clearly. The other man responded.

"Yeah, it's fine. It's one of the new girls; she's just lost."

The voice over the radio came back: "Well where the hell is Thompson?"

The guy on the radio walked away while I continued trying to charm Dwayne Johnson over here.

"This place is so big, how do you ever know where you're going?" I asked, taking the crook of his arm and walking toward the door.

"It is confusing at first," he said softening to my touch.

"Where were you trying to go?" he asked.

"Oh honey, I am starving. I think the boys upstairs forget that some of us need real food. I can't seem to find the kitchen anywhere."

He smiled. We walked down the hallway back to the stairs. The guy with the radio was yelling at a young man holding a cup of coffee. I guessed he was supposed to be standing guard.

"...and then it's on the left, sweetheart." The big guy had been giving me directions to the kitchen, but I wasn't listening.

"Oh okay, thank you so much," I said.

"Be careful not to come down this way again, you could get into a lot of trouble," he said.

"Oh, I won't, honey I promise." I winked at him and hurried up the steps quickly. I didn't breathe easy until I was through the door and inside the kitchen. I figured I should go there for safety sake.

I decided just to go back to my room so I couldn't get into any more trouble. On my way back I started thinking about the two men I'd seen in the cells downstairs. The man in the cell with the flashing lights, I felt like I knew who he was, like I'd seen him before. It took me a moment to put together what was going on inside that room. I remembered when I had taken Li home from the hospital, he pretty much ran inside and told me the motion lights were UV. He said they were a vampire repellant and were sometimes used for torture. So, that man was being tortured, but for what...to get information, as a punishment? Then it hit me; I knew where I'd seen him. He was one of the seed hunters I'd followed here. He was probably being punished for his carelessness. But what about the other guy lying on the floor in the first hallway? He wasn't being tortured by lights. I wondered what the story was with him. Maybe he was already dead.

"So who killed him?" I heard someone say. It startled me, and I looked up. It was René; I just stared at her.

"Well come on now," she said in her thick accent. "Who killed him, was it the mayor? It was the mayor wasn't it?"

It took me a minute to realize she wasn't talking about the guy downstairs but the TV show we had been watching together earlier.

"Oh, no it was actually the secretary. She and the mayor were having an affair, and the brother caught them."

"It's always the quiet ones," she said. "Oh, hey it's supposed to be real nice out today, you want to go sit by the pool later?" she asked.

"Outside?" I said and then realized how stupid that must sound, of course outside. "I mean, we're allowed to go outside?"

She looked at me puzzled. "Yes, of course. It may be a little cold, but we can get in the water too if ya want. Do you have a suit? I have one you can borrow if you don't."

"This is all I have," I said holding out my arms."

"Oh honey," she said shaking her head, "come with me."

René's room was really small compared to Wu's. She had a small bed in the corner, a small table, and a little couch, and that was it. Her bathroom was a decent size, though, and then I saw her closet. It was massive, almost as big as her room! I followed her inside, yes, inside, it was a walk-in. She started randomly pulling things off the rack and handing them to me.

"You can have this, and this, and this…"

I ended up with over a dozen things draped over my arms.

"Come on, you can try them on."

She had a couple full-length mirrors in one corner of her room. She threw all the clothes on the bed and started dressing me up like a full-sized doll. A few of the things didn't fit. René was skinnier than I was, and I was taller than her. I was a little embarrassed by being dressed and undressed by another woman, but René didn't seem to give two thoughts about it.

"What size are those, sugah, 'bout a 36C? I might have something in here to fit you."

I really didn't think she had anything small enough for me; her boobs were huge, not like Pam Anderson fake huge, but definitely bigger than mine. Like I said, this girl looked like a model. She came back with a black lace bra that actually looked like it might fit. I ended up with a bra, a pair of Capri sweats, a couple pair of shorts, (none of her pants would fit me) half a dozen shirts, and a couple dresses.

"Do you not have any shoes, either?" she asked.

"No, I have nothing but what I'm wearing now."

"Oh honey, that's a downright crime!"

"You don't have to give me anything else," I said, "I feel bad for you giving me all this."

"Oh don't, my birthday is the 27th, and I always go on a massive shopping spree. I'd end up throwing half this stuff out anyway. Bobby takes me down to the Concord Mall every year for my birthday."

I loved how she didn't call him Bobb-ee but Bobb-eh.

We spent the next few hours looking through clothes and shoes. René brushed out my knotted, tangled mess of hair because I didn't have a brush. I felt like a twelve-year-old having a slumber party. She'd given me clothes, a hairbrush, and deodorant, but I was still shoeless. I wore a size seven, and she was a five and a half. We agreed to meet up later in the evening when it warmed up and go outside. I almost forgot what kind of place I was in, that I was being held prisoner by vampires who dragged people here against their will to be turned into vampires. I had a feeling René thought this more of a fraternity house than the vampire changing prison that I saw it as. I wondered if she really knew what went on here.

I went back to my room and slept through the afternoon. Later, I went back down to René's room at the time we'd agreed on. Her room was on the bottom floor right next to the secondary staircase. She met me in the hallway, and we went through a door, down a short plain hallway, and to another door. She pressed a button beside the door that made a buzzing sound then she turned around and did a wiggly finger wave to a camera mounted on the wall. A second later we heard a click, and she opened the door. Oh! It was a sun room. A bright, glorious warm sunroom! I hadn't seen the sun in days! I just stood there looking up trying to absorb every drop.

René laughed at me. "Come on, girl, you need some outside time."

I did! It felt wonderful to be outside. I felt like I'd been locked up in that house for a year already. We sat outside talking for hours. I didn't want to go back in, but René said she had to but promised we'd do it again soon.

The rest of the week went quickly. I spent my nights with Wu pretending to have sex, and my afternoons with René outside or in the sunroom. I was surprised at how easily we were able to go from inside to outside by just that little buzzer on the door. I assumed the security guys controlled the door lock. I wondered if it would be as easy if I wasn't with René. I tried a little experiment one day and "accidentally" left the magazine I borrowed from René in the sunroom. After she and I had parted ways, I went back to see if I could get it. I went to the door and hit the buzzer and waited. I heard the click and opened the door. A newfound freedom washed over me. I got my magazine and walked out of the sunroom into the open. I stood there for a few moments to see if anyone would show up telling me to go back inside, but they didn't.

I stood there in the September breeze. Oh, what a difference a year can make in your life. One year ago I didn't know vampires existed. Look at me now, look what's all happened in the course of one year. Now I was being held captive by vampires inside a mansion in North Carolina. My week was up; we were going to question Arlo about my release again. If he said no, maybe I could escape. I decided to press my luck. I walked out into the yard and over to the fence and waited. No one came rushing out to stop me; no one yelled at me to get away from there, nothing. I could climb this fence if I needed to. It wasn't barbed wire or anything; it was the creepy rod iron you saw around cemeteries. I'd been standing here a few minutes. I could've climbed it by now and been running into the woods behind the house. I could make it as long as I left during daylight hours so the vamps wouldn't come after me. All I'd have to do is run to the nearest pay phone and call Brian or Li; they would come get me. I could do it early in the day, so I could be long gone, back home in Tennessee before the vampires even woke up.

I wondered if René would want to leave, too. She seemed really happy here, though, and I couldn't chance her selling me out and telling anyone that I was escaping. Wu could hold his own. He said he could leave if he really insisted on it. He was sticking around to see if he could discover Arlo's secret motives for keeping him here, so I wasn't worried about him. Okay, I had a plan. If Arlo didn't say I could leave when we met with him, I was going to escape. I would jump the fence and run.

SIX

I needed somewhere I could think and make plans. Somewhere I wasn't being watched on camera. All these security cameras were making me crazy! I hated the thought of someone watching my every move. I hated not having any privacy. I couldn't concentrate. There had to be somewhere I could go to think. I knew there were cameras outside. Wu's room was out, and the hallways. Maybe one of the less important rooms might not have cameras. The laundry room perhaps, there was no need for a camera in there, right. I walked back inside looking for a place hidden from camera view. Inside the small hallway, if I stood right up against the wall the camera probably couldn't see me. I didn't want to stand there, though. I wanted to sit down and really think about this and make some solid plans. I scoured the house, hallway after hallway, room after room noticing where all the cameras were. It'd be useful information to know anyway. The laundry rooms didn't have cameras, but they were too noisy with the machines going. Then I saw the utility room, perfect.

It was a decent sized room with shelves everywhere. Filled with mops, brooms, various supplies, and I briefly wondered who cleaned this house. Did they have a maid? I'd never seen anyone cleaning. Focus Em, escape. I turned a bucket upside down and sat on it. I could still hear the rumbling of the dryers next door, but it wasn't distractingly loud. Okay, so if Arlo refused to let me go I will wait till daylight, probably around noon. René usually is asleep then so running into her won't be a problem, and by noon it's warm enough that going outside wouldn't seem odd. I was going to need shoes. There was no way I could hop the fence and run off into the woods barefoot. Maybe one of the other girls had some that would fit me. I'd seen a few other girls walking around besides

Jackie, at least one other pregnant woman. Arlo was running a regular seed factory over here.

If all else failed, I could stuff some toilet paper in the front of Wu's shoes. Wu would be waking up here soon. I wanted to go over this whole plan with him, of course. I couldn't decide if I should call Li or Brian once I got far enough away. If I called Brian, I would have some explaining to do. I could catch a taxi, boy that would be a crazy expensive ride. I couldn't think. I guess the sun had set because I could hear people stirring around. I could hear them talking in the laundry room through a big silver pipe thing in the wall. I looked around for something to stuff in it to mute their conversation so I could think, but then their conversation caught my attention:

Guy 1: So why don't they just go kill his grandfather?

Guy 2: You know as well as I do they can't do that, he's a seed, we don't kill seeds.

Guy 1: So Arlo is just going to keep this guy here making excuses till the old man dies? That could take forever. He'll catch on for sure.

Guy 2: Kevin said the guy was seriously old and feeble, that's why they didn't just grab him, too.

Guy 1: Yeah, one old geezer vamp is enough.

Guy 2: Shhh dude, they may not kill seeds, but they will kill us Ectypes without a second thought, and you know that. That mouth of yours is going to get you in serious trouble one day.

They were talking about Wu. That's why Arlo was keeping him here? He was waiting for Li to die, but why? Then I started worrying about this Kevin guy. The seed hunters had obviously been casing the shop, what if the ones that took Wu that night recognized me? I was hoping those guys would give me more clues as to why Arlo wanted Li dead before he let Wu go, but they started talking about the upcoming football season. I planned on waiting for them to leave before I left but they just went on talking, so I quietly and carefully got up, opened the door, and slipped out. Then I hurried to Wu's room.

"Hey, you're up," I said. "Let's go do that laundry now, okay? Before everybody else gets down there and hogs up the machines."

"Yeah, okay," he said knowing I was up to something. I started grabbing random clothes here and there, dirty or not, and we went downstairs. I'd been in the west wing, Arlo's wing, when I overheard the guys talking. So, we went down to the east wing laundry room. Thankfully it was empty. I stuffed all the clothes into a dryer and turned it on for the cover noise.

"Holy freaking crap, Wu, I just found out why Arlo won't let you leave...well, sort of," I said in a whisper.

"How?"

"I was in the utility room and overheard two guys talking."

Wu gave me a strange look.

"How's not important, listen! Arlo wants to keep you here until Li dies."

I barely got the words out when Wu grabbed me and kissed me, he kissed me hard and passionately. He picked me up and set me on top of the dryer and started making out hot and heavy. I'd been a part of this crazy lifestyle too long because without even looking I knew that someone had walked in, and I knew Wu wanted things to look hot enough that they wouldn't stick around to see what happened next.

"Geez, get a room," I heard a guy say then we were alone again. Like nothing just happened at all, we picked up our conversation.

"Why till Umpa dies?" he asked.

"I have no idea, but they said they couldn't just kill him because they can't kill seeds. So, they are just going to keep you here until he dies."

"But why?" he asked again.

"I don't know. I've got something else to tell you, too."

I went on to tell him my escape plan, only having to stop one more time to make out enough to make someone else leave.

"I don't know, Em, that sounds kind of risky. Let's just hope Arlo will keep his word and let you go."

More people came walking in, but we were pretty much done talking, so we left.

Later that evening René came and got me to dress me up like her life-sized Barbie once again. She was dressed up herself in a tight red dress. She looked like Jessica

Rabbit with a little bit of Marilyn Monroe thrown in. She was gorgeous, and I admit, I was a little bit jealous of her. I wanted to be her; she was so fun and full of life. Her personality was intoxicating. You just wanted to be around her. She dressed me up in a lacy black dress and curled my hair. She was putting makeup on me when Mickey came in and pulled her away again. I got the feeling Mickey was the low man on the totem pole because he seemed to be the go get 'em man around here.

After René left, I went back to Wu's room.

"Wow, Em," he said as he walked over to me. "You walk in here looking like that, and I might not be pretending next time," he whispered as he kissed me on the cheek. He stepped back and winked at me, and I blushed. I'd been naked with Wu half a dozen times now and made out with him countless times, but I actually blushed at that. We went downstairs like most nights (early mornings) before bed. Arlo and a small crowd of others were in the piano lounge in the west wing. Someone was playing the piano, and René was singing.

She had a beautiful voice. I felt a little sad that she was pulled away from chasing her dreams as a singer to come here. She was great! It really didn't seem fair to the rest of the women of the world for her to be the entire package that she was. She was singing a song I didn't recognize and walking around the room seductively yet playfully singing to everyone. She even booped me on the nose when she walked by, and I laughed.

"She's so amazing; I just love her," I said to Wu.

"Really?" he asked. "I thought you detested hookers? I was surprised you took to her like you did."

My mouth dropped open. René was a hooker?

"Noooo," I said. "What?! No."

"Yeah, Em, what did you think she did here?"

"I just thought she was Bobby's girlfriend," I replied.

"Well she is, and Mickey's, and Franco's, and Jesse's..."

"Yeah I get it, oh not Arlo's," I whispered. "Please tell me not Arlo, too."

"Shhh, no," he said smiling. "Arlo doesn't believe in recreational sex; he does it for procreation only, the continuation of the species."

I shivered at the thought.

I couldn't believe René was a hooker, but I thought so highly of her, she just might change my opinion of hookers. Now, she was singing a hauntingly beautiful rendition of Summertime and the whole room had gone quiet to listen. After the song Wu and I walked over to where Arlo was sitting.

"Ah, brother Wu, Miss Emina." He nodded. I hated that he used my full name, but Wu told me that Arlo hated nicknames or the shortening of names. Everyone here was called by their birth-given name, you couldn't be Jon or Chris here, you were Jonathan or Christopher.

"The week is over, I'd like to discuss Emina's release," Wu said.

"Let's discuss it in the morning," Arlo said. "René's singing is such a treat; I won't discuss business now."

So he was going to put off my leaving just like he had Wu's. He was never going to let either of us leave. Well, my mind was made up. It was around three a.m. so in approximately nine hours I would jump the fence and leave this place. I wondered if Wu would leave too, or if he still wanted to stick around to find out why Arlo wanted his grandfather dead. I think Wu was just about to argue with Arlo and insist they work out the conditions of my release, but Mickey walked in with a message.

"There's an Ectype outside requesting refuge from the sun," he said.

"How long till sunrise?" Arlo asked.

"Three hours thirty-nine minutes," Mickey answered.

"Age?" Arlo asked.

"He says he's two hundred and seventy."

"Alright, show him in," Arlo said. "What is his name?"

"Bohuslav."

Wu and I both looked at each other. There was no way there was another Ectype out there that was two hundred and seventy years old named Bohuslav. This was Bo! My Bo! Did he know I was here? Had he come to rescue me? I bet Li told him I'd gone missing. I imagined life back home many times with Li worried sick. Brian wondering for days if I was mad at him then becoming worried and maybe even reporting me missing to the police. I wasn't sure what Bo's presence did to my escape plans. I didn't know why he was here, what he would do? Maybe there was going to be another epic battle like what happened to the seed hunters that broke into my house. Maybe Bo would walk through the door, give Wu a nod and they would just start slinging vampires everywhere!

Bo walked in, and I had to ignore the urge to run to him and throw my arms around him. I hadn't seen him in almost six months now. He looked amazing in a dark green sweater and his usual black pants. He looked like he hadn't shaved since he'd left, and the stubble was a very good look for him, although he looked exhausted. I wanted to go to him and comfort him. I was suddenly very conscious of my close proximity to Wu. Bo looked at us and looked down. We were holding hands. Oh, awkward! I tried to let go of Wu's hand, feeling like I was cheating on Bo even though we weren't together anymore. Wu squeezed it and wouldn't let go. He moved around behind me and put both arms around me resting his chin on my shoulder.

"I know it's hard, Em, but we have to keep up our charade. Don't do anything to compromise your life. Stick with the plan," he whispered to me.

I hadn't seen Bo in months, but it wasn't long enough to get over him. Seeing him resurrected every feeling I had toward him: love, hate, resentment, lust. They were all there.

Bo walked up to Arlo. "Thank you for your hospitality," he said.

Well, so much for a vampire slinging battle, I thought.

"You're most welcome, Bohuslav. An Ectype of your age is rare; you must be a resourceful and adaptive man."

"Yes, I am. It doesn't hurt that I can kick some serious ass, too."

"Indeed," Arlo said shifting positions in his chair, seeming on edge now. "Come, sit. Tell us about yourself," Arlo suggested.

"Actually if you don't mind, I'm very tired. I just want to sleep."

"Very well," Arlo said. "Would you like a feeder or some female company perhaps?" he asked pointing toward René.

No, no, no, no, no, I silently protested.

"Just a feeder, thank you," Bo said.

I breathed out a sigh of relief that must have been somewhat noticeable because Wu tightened his arms around me.

"Franco will take care of you," Arlo said.

I remembered Franco, the man who dragged me upstairs supposedly to my death. I wondered if he was going to drag some other poor girl to Bo's room to her death. I wasn't exactly sure what a feeder was. I got a chill thinking about it. Bo turned to follow Franco and stopped in front of me.

"What about this girl?" he asked looking me up and down. Wu tightened his grip around me and was about to speak.

"I'm sorry, this girl belongs to Wu," Arlo said. "...and he is quite adamant about keeping her to himself I'm afraid," Arlo answered. "Oh and Bohuslav, there are a few house rules..." Arlo started, but I didn't hear them because Wu was leading me out of the room.

"Come on," he whispered.

"Where are we going?" I asked.

"We're going to talk to Bo."

Wu led us across the foyer and down the English hunter hallway. We stood there at the end and waited just a moment before Franco led Bo down toward us. We made sure Bo saw us before we turned the corner.

"How did you know Franco would bring him down here?" I asked.

"Arlo doesn't trust him, so I figured he'd be put as far away from his own room as possible."

Wu peeked around the corner every few seconds. Franco had left. A few minutes passed, and he came back with a girl, the "feeder" I guessed.

"What's a feeder?" I asked while we were waiting.

"It's a person continually used for their blood. They are never drained, but are kept around basically as a readily available snack."

Okay, that wasn't as bad as I thought. The girl came right back out and headed back the way she came. Bo came out a moment later and headed toward us.

"Laundry room," Wu told me before Bo had completely caught up to us, and I headed that direction. Luckily there was no one in there. It was getting close to dawn, so there weren't many people stirring. I slipped inside and waited, Wu came in next, then Bo.

"That pompous prick sent me a diseased whore," Bo fumed.

"Hey," I said. "I thought vampires don't get mad," I smiled.

Bo walked over and pulled me to him. It lasted far too long to be a friendly hug. I may never understand this man. I took in his familiar smell and the feel of his arms and chest. I thought I was making progress in getting over him, but there in his arms, I knew I was back at square one now. He let me go and cradled my face in both hands.

"Did they hurt you? If they hurt you, by God I'll rip out their throats, every last one of them."

"No, no, they tried to. They were going to kill me, but Wu saved me."

Bo let go of me and also hugged Wu. "I'm sorry I failed to protect you, my friend."

It was such a tender moment I almost teared up.

"How did you find us?" Wu asked.

"Process of elimination, this is the second place I looked. I went to Atlanta first," Bo said.

"So now what?" I asked.

"We stick to your plan, Em," Wu said. "You go ahead and jump the fence today and lay low until nightfall. Then you and Bo can meet and leave together."

"What about you?" Bo asked Wu. "You're not leaving?"

"I'm going to stay awhile longer; I need to…"

Wu stopped mid-sentence, and we turned to see what he was staring at. There in the doorway stood a man. Wu recognized him, and so did I.

"Oh no," I said. I don't think Bo knew who the man was until I breathed the words, "the one that got away."

The man took off down the hallway, and I guess out of instinct Bo took off after him. This was the man that had broken into my house looking for Wu last year. I hadn't seen him around the house since I'd been here, and I guessed Wu hadn't either. Clearly, the man recognized us. Wu had fought him, and I'd stabbed him with my baseball bat. He knew the three of us were together, and I guessed he was on his way to tell Arlo who we all really were.

"Go NOW, Em! You have to go now!" Wu said then took off after the man. I stood there in shock for a minute. I had to will my legs to move. I was worried before about having to jump the fence and run without shoes; now I was going to have to do it without shoes, in a short lacey dress, and before dawn...not the best odds. I hurried to the door that led to the sunroom. I pressed the buzzer and waited, nothing. I turned around and looked at the camera and forced myself a fake smile then pressed it again, again nothing. I tried opening the door anyway, and of course, it wouldn't open. I pressed the buzzer two more times. They weren't going to let me out. They had let me out without René before, maybe because it wasn't daylight. Maybe baldy had already gotten to Arlo and told him.

Okay, new plan. I'd go find René and ask her if she wants to go watch the sunrise. Maybe they would let me out if she's with me. I stopped by her room first, but she wasn't there. I really hoped she wasn't still with Arlo in the lounge. I planned to check all of her usual hangouts but just down the hall from René's room two men grabbed me and dragged me back to Arlo. René wasn't still in this room, but Bo and Wu were, along with baldy and several other men.

"Ah, here we are..." Arlo said as the men dragged me across the room. "...one big happy lying scheming family. What did the three of you think you could do?"

I could see Wu's disappointment when they brought me in; he'd hoped I'd gotten away. He wasn't being held, but Bo had a man on each side of him holding his arms.

"Let them go, Arlo," Wu said.

"Oh, I don't think so, brother," He replied.

Arlo motioned for the men to bring me to him and he grabbed my arm with his long, cold fingers that made my skin crawl.

"You will let her go!" Wu said in a commanding voice looking fierce. Bo struggled against the two men that held him and rattled off cussing threats. Wu held up his hand to stop him.

"I am an Antecedent, this is my woman, and you cannot harm her!"

"Breathe in the air, brother Wu," Arlo said in a spectral voice. "She's about to bleed; I can smell it. So either you failed to impregnate her, or you were trying to deceive me. Both are grounds to revoke her protection. Now because of your lying and scheming ways, you will watch her die." With that Arlo plunged his fangs into the back of my neck.

Bo let out a booming howl and went absolutely ballistic. Two more men had to come hold him down. Three men stepped in front of Wu who had taken a couple steps toward me.

"I'll kill you for this! I'll kill you!" Bo screamed.

"Wait! Stop!" Wu said. "Let them go and I'll stay here. I'll stay, no questions asked. I'll stay, just let them go. Please."

Arlo hesitated a moment still drinking from me.

"Fine," Arlo said pulling his teeth out of my neck. I felt so dizzy. "It's too late for this one, anyway," he said letting go of the grip he had on me. I felt the room spin as I fell to the floor, and everything went dark.

EIGHT

"Wake up, Em, please, please wake up." I opened my heavy eyelids to see Wu carrying me.

"I think I'm dying, Wu," I said weakly.

"Yes, Em, you are." Wu's face twisted with pain. Could vampires cry, I wondered.

"It may be too late, Em, I don't know if I can save you."

Wu quickly and covertly bit his finger and stuck it in my mouth. Blood trickled down my throat as he carried me outside. I didn't know where Bo was, if he was alive, or if Arlo would really let him go or not. Wu carried me to the front gate. I saw two men shove Bo out past the gate.

"I don't know if she'll make it," Wu said to Bo. "I don't know if it was enough," he whispered. Wu handed me off to Bo then he leaned down. I thought he was going to kiss me, but when his lips met mine, he spilled a mouthful of blood into my mouth. He must have bitten his own tongue. My instinct was to pull away and spit it out, but I just didn't have the strength. I swallowed the mouthful of blood and once again everything went black.

"I didn't expect you back anywhere near this soon," I heard a familiar voice say. I was hovering on the edge of consciousness. "Oh my God, what happened? You were supposed to save her!"

Brian? Were we back home in Tennessee? Had I been unconscious that long?

"I tried to save her," Bo said, his voice sounding solemn, "I failed."

"Is she dead?"

"No, not yet, but I'm not sure she'll make it through the night."

"So let's take her to a hospital!" Brian said.

"We can't."

"Why the hell not?" Brian asked, Bo didn't respond but must have given Brian a look. "Are you freaking kidding me?! I wish she'd never met you guys!"

"Wu saved her life! She would've been dead a week ago if it wasn't for him, and he may have just saved her again. Only time will tell. Now come on, the sun will be up soon. We have to go."

I woke up shivering. I was so cold! I pulled my legs to me and wrapped my arms around myself. I'm naked, lying on a cold hard floor. Why am I naked?

"Bo?"

"He's in the trunk; it's daylight. Are you ok, Em?" Brian asked me.

"I'm so cold, Bri, where are my clothes?"

"I'm sorry, Em, Bo said we should take them off."

"I'm cold," I repeated.

Brian took off his flannel shirt and sat down beside me. He pulled me onto his lap and cradled me like a baby. He spread his shirt across me, and I was out again.

I died right there that day on the floor in Brian's arms. I died, but Wu's blood was able to bring me back from death. I must have had just enough of his blood to turn me. I wonder if he hadn't given me that one last mouthful if maybe I would have just laid there and died completely in my best friend's arms.

When I opened my eyes, everything looked perfectly clear, crisper and sharper than ever before. I felt calm, surprisingly so. My hearing seemed keener. I could hear cars passing by outside. I heard water dripping in the distance. I heard Bo's voice.

"I told you that would happen if she lived," I heard Bo say. What would happen? I was currently overwhelmed by my senses. It was like sensory overload. Sight, hearing, smell...yes smell, and it was something horrible, like sewage.

"I don't care," Brian said. "I'm just glad she's alive."

I looked down at my body. I was still naked, but I was covered in filth. Vomit, urine, feces. It was all my own. I think maybe I should have been horribly embarrassed, but I wasn't really.

"What happened?" I asked.

"You got mixed up with all these damn vampires, and now you are one," Brian said.

"Arlo nearly killed you," Bo said shooting Brian a look. "Wu gave you his blood so you wouldn't die."

"Why am I covered in filth?"

"Your body has changed over, Em, you're a vampire now. Your system has been purged of everything human. You're one of us now."

"Where are we?" I looked around and saw nothing but cement floor and walls on all sides.

"A parking garage of an old office building, we had to take shelter from the sun. Em, the sun will kill you now, you must avoid it at all costs. One beam of sunlight is all it takes; you will catch fire, and you will die," Bo warned.

I must have seemed totally out of it. I stood up and just took everything in. Brian tried to hand me a bottle of water and napkins, but I was too enthralled by my surroundings to notice. Every little thing seemed to catch my attention. Great, like I wasn't borderline ADD already.

"It's as close as you can get to a shower right now," Brian said, and I noticed what he was trying to hand me.

"Bo, is she okay?" Brian asked like I wasn't standing right in front of them.

"Yes," he smiled. It takes some getting use to."

"I'll help you, Em," Brian said pouring the water and wiping me off. It reminded me of the time I had the stomach flu, and Brian came over to take care of me. I was glad I had my human memories still. Bo said so many times he didn't remember being human, but I guess it's easier to remember what you were yesterday than what you were three hundred years ago.

Brian cleaned me up and helped me put my clothes back on while Bo stood there watching. Being a vampire hadn't changed his attraction to my body. I could see it in his eyes. Now I just was, how had he put it? oh yeah, 'an unfavorable temperature.' Brian was now trying to clean my fluids off his arm and pants. He had held me all day anyway. I hugged him. "Thank you, Bri."

I took a moment to survey my emotions. I was calm, very calm, but I still felt like me. I thought about Brian as I looked at him. I studied his face, his eyes, brown on the verge of hazel. I think I felt the same about him as I always had. A brotherly type love, admiration, complete trust all as before. I looked at Bo and did the same. I noticed all the things I'd dwelled on when he walked into the mansion last night, how the green sweater set off his dark eyes, his stubble, his dark hair. I felt love, longing, and passion. I walked over to him and kissed him, purely research, of course. I pulled back to look at him.

"Bohuslav Pavlock, you're a liar. I still feel love, I still feel."

"Is that what you're doing?" He laughed, amused at my careful analysis of them.

"Perhaps it's different if you loved someone while you were still human then turned. Maybe new love is impossible to find as a vampire," he said.

"Yes, and perhaps you're full of absolute crap."

"Ah, but tell me something, Em, if I were to walk out of your life right now, today, how would you feel?"

I thought about that a few moments. I tried to picture it in my head. I was pleasantly surprised. I smiled.

"Frankly, Scarlet, I don't think I'd give a damn."

Bo smiled. "...and there you have it."

Okay, I liked this whole vampire thing. Totally relaxed, aware, unfazed by life's little problems, I could get used to this.

"Em, you need to eat, you'll feel much better," Bo said. "Do you have a preference for your first meal? Dog...human? We are too far into the city for much wild game."

"I don't want to kill anything!" I protested.

"Ah, Em, you do realize that you are a vampire now, right? You have to kill; you have to eat," Bo said.

I put my hands on both sides of my head. I was dizzy, and my head hurt.

"What's wrong with my head, Bo, I thought I was supposed to be invincible now?"

"Oh yeah, I forgot about that part," Bo said. "You're going to get a migraine, but it should only last about a day then you'll be right as rain.

"A migraine? Why?"

"You're not used to seeing everything, hearing everything; your body is still adjusting. It really would help if you eat something. It doesn't have to be human, Em, blood is blood, but you must eat."

"What about a cat, Em, you hate cats," Brian suggested.

"No!" Bo said. "Cats are far more trouble than they're worth. They have so little blood that it's not worth getting your face all scratched up."

"But why do I have to kill? Can't I find a feeder like at the mansion?"

"Yeah, I suppose, but it will take awhile to find someone trustworthy enough to keep our secret."

"What's a feeder?" Brian asked.

"It's a walking blood bank basically. They are never drained, but small amounts of blood are taken from them at a time," Bo answered.

"...and it doesn't hurt them? They won't turn into a vampire or anything?" Brian asked. He clearly hadn't been given the whole story.

"No, they aren't harmed at all, no more dangerous than donating blood."

"...and blood will make Em feel better?" Brian asked.

"Yes," Bo answered.

Brian walked over and stuck his arm in front of my face.

"Here, but please don't accidentally kill me in the process."

I looked at Brian stunned. There really wasn't anything he wouldn't do for me. I looked at Bo waiting for his okay, though; I wasn't sure why.

"Go ahead," Bo said. "I'll tell you when to stop."

I hadn't thought about it yet, but I ran my tongue over my teeth, I found pointed fangs, much sharper than Bo's. I assumed his had been worn down over time because Wu's were also very sharp. I liked the dulled ones much better. These scared me a little. They were so sharp and seemed so deadly. I grabbed Brian's arm and brought it up to my mouth. This whole thing seemed so alien to me. I wasn't sure where I should bite him. I didn't want to bite his wrist because I was afraid the blood might come out too quickly, so I went halfway down his forearm. I moved to the side of his tattoo; I didn't want to leave a scar and mess up his dragon. I bit down, and blood filled my mouth. A rush of heat, warmth, and energy, came over me like a warm cup of coffee. I liked it…a little too much.

"Stop!" Bo said. Had I been biting anyone else I would've found it hard to stop, but I would never do anything to hurt Brian. I felt like I'd only started drinking two seconds ago, and I wanted more but was able to stop. I pulled back and looked at Brian to make sure he was okay, he was.

"The wound will heal faster if you lick it," Bo told me.

Although it was a little weird, I licked Brian's arm a few times where I bit him.

"You okay?" I asked Brian still holding onto his arm.

"Is it okay that I was totally turned on by that?" he asked.

"Oh, Brian!" I scolded, letting go of his arm.

"Just keepin' it real yo." He smiled.

I was about to say something else but a fire truck's siren close by made me cover my ears and wince at the pain in my head.

"Let's get you home, Em," Bo said. "You may want to ride in the trunk."

"What? No," I said. "I don't want to ride for hours in the trunk!"

"And you don't have to!" Brian interrupted.

"It will help with the sensory overload," Bo suggested.

"Listen here, pimp, she doesn't want to," Brian said combatively.

"And you listen to me…pimp," Bo said mockingly. "You don't have a clue what she's going through right now, but I do, so why don't you be a good little blood bank and go sit down and let the immortals talk."

I knew the look Brian had on his face, he was mad. Brian was the most laid back person I knew, but Bo had a way of getting to him.

"Would you two stop," I said getting in between them and pushing them both. "I'll lie in the backseat, and if it gets to be too much I'll get in the trunk. I'm a big girl now; I can make my own decisions. I really don't know how in the world the two of you worked together long enough to come up with a rescue plan."

"Your friend is annoyingly persistent, that's how," Bo said as we got into the car.

"I wouldn't have had to be so persistent if you weren't so stubborn," Brian shot back.

It was going to be a long ride home. Once we started driving, I understood what Bo meant about sensory overload. I noticed everything! Every little thing was so crisp and clear. I noticed details I never had before. I noticed everything, and it made my head ache even more. It only took about fifteen minutes before I had to lie down and close my eyes to block out all the things I was seeing. When I did, the sounds seemed to magnify. Cars, horns honking, dogs barking. I could hone in on them and tell which direction they were coming from and could almost guess how far away. This was maddening. I needed something to focus my attention on to keep it from bouncing everywhere.

"So how did you two get together to rescue me? When did you get back from Lithuania, Bo?"

"That's where your friend's annoying persistence comes in. I was there when he emailed me and told me you were missing and insisted that I come back and help find you. Fifty-seven emails later I flew back to help. I figured it'd be the only way to get him to shut up."

It was funny how Bo always called Brian 'my friend,' he rarely called him by his name.

"How did you get Bo's email address?" I asked.

"I kinda hijacked your laptop when you went missing. I knew something was wrong after about two days, your mail piled up and Bacon was starving. I didn't want to call the police because I knew you were mixed up with some shady stuff from the way you'd been acting. So I played detective. I went down to the antique shop and talked to that old Chinese guy, and I started emailing Bo. I knew something bad happened, and I figured your boss would be able to get to the bottom of it faster than I could. A few days of bugging him to come and help, one trip to Atlanta and one to Charlotte, and here we are."

No wonder Bo looked tired. He probably hadn't had a decent day's sleep since he left Lithuania. I tried doing the math in my head of how long he must have been back and how long I'd been gone, but I couldn't concentrate. I think I'd been in the mansion eight days, maybe nine. I wasn't sure. I'd lost track of time while I was there. My days and nights were completely mixed up, and I wasn't even sure what day it was now.

"Tell me about the mansion, Em," Bo said. "What happened?"

I went on to tell him everything I knew about the house, the security, and Arlo. I told them about the things I'd seen in the basement. I told them everything.

"I should've known you'd go off looking to save Wu by yourself," Bo said.

So, he thought that's what I did? Well, that sounded a lot better than me running off to be changed into a vampire because I was upset and depressed. The words of my aunt echoed in my head, "Don't do something permanently stupid because you're temporarily upset." Yeah, they could just go on thinking I was a one-man rescue team, stupid yes, but not as pathetic as the real reasons were.

"How did you find him?" Bo asked.

"I started hanging around the auctions, and I followed the seed hunters back there."

"Hold up," Brian said. "Y'all lost me. What's a seed hunter?"

The rest of the trip back Bo and I filled Brian in on the vampire world. It felt good to tell him everything. I hated hiding things from him all this time. I told him all I knew, and Bo filled in the holes on the things I wasn't sure about. Brian took it exceptionally well. I didn't know how much he'd seen and heard already, but he wasn't at all skeptical of what we were telling him.

"Brian, you seem to be taking this all really well."

As soon as I said it, Bo busted out laughing, but I had no idea why.

"What? What did I miss?" I asked.

"This dude bit into a freakin' terrier right in front of me, Em! Bit into it, drank it, then dropped it at my feet!"

Bo hadn't stopped laughing yet. He was completely amused with himself.

"Bo!" I scolded.

"He wouldn't have believed me otherwise," Bo chuckled.

That was probably true.

We pulled up to the antique store, and it was a welcomed sight. Brian got out and lit a cigarette immediately. I wasn't sure if he hadn't smoked during the drive out of courtesy or if maybe Bo had threatened his life if he smoked in his car.

"How am I getting home, Bo?" I asked.

I didn't know if he wanted me to take his car or if I should have Brian drop me off.

"You can't go home, Em, you can't sleep there. You have no protection from the sun."

"Oh," I said disappointedly. I really wanted to be in my own house, in my own room, and all by myself after a week at the mansion always being watched.

"You'll stay here with me," Bo said.

"I'm going to head out, Em, text me, okay," Brian said stomping out his cigarette.

"I can't," I said. "My phone is gone. I left it in my purse, in my car. I don't have my phone, my wallet, my driver's license, credit cards, nothing. It's all gone."

Brian hugged me. I took in the heightened smell that defined him, smoke and cologne. It was a familiar comforting smell.

"It'll be alright, Em, I'm just glad you're okay...well, mostly okay. I'll come back tomorrow night," he said getting into his Jeep.

"Don't you have to work?" I asked.

"Ahhh no, I don't work there anymore," he said oddly, and I'd be willing to bet he lost his job because he had taken too much time off looking for me. He drove off before I could say anything.

"Come on," Bo said leading me inside.

It felt absolutely wonderful to shower. Brushing my teeth was a new experience; I stood there looking at my fangs for a long while. I stood in front of the mirror looking at my body as well. I think I'd lost a few pounds at the mansion. Food was a little scarce there. My skin seemed tighter, thicker somehow, and I'm not going to lie, I think my boobs were a little perkier, too. I looked just a little different, but I couldn't place how exactly. Maybe my body wasn't different at all. Perhaps I was seeing everything vividly with new eyes, eyes that noticed every detail and my new mind that didn't seem to be quite as sensitive to emotion. Bo opened the door and put some clothes for me on top of the towel cabinet.

"Do I look different to you?" I asked not embarrassed at all that I was standing there naked, but Bo had seen me naked many times before.

"No," he paused looking at me. "You're as breathtaking as you've always been," he said and ducked back out of the room.

I put on the clothes that Bo brought me, boxers and a t-shirt. I didn't think I was ever going to wear my own clothes again. It was just after midnight so I thought Bo would be up for awhile, but he laid down in bed beside me.

"I'm glad you're safe, Em."

"It took three days and that many emails to get you to come and look for me, though?"

"I booked my flights after the first email. It just took me that long to get back. Same old Em, you believe what you deduce in your own mind, not what actually is. That hasn't changed."

He brushed his hand through my hair a few times.

"Now get some sleep. Your life is going to be different now, Em. I'll teach you all that I can, but you're going to have to do things a little differently now. Mainly you're going to have to learn to kill."

I awoke curled up next to Bo, and I felt like nothing had changed. I nuzzled my face into his neck and kissed it.

"Are you ready to start your vampire training?" he asked me.

"I guess," I said. I really wasn't ready to get out of bed yet.

"Lesson number one: Don't fall in love, love is torture."

Wow, I knew Bo was an apathetic man, but this took me by surprise a little.

"Wait a minute; I thought vampires weren't capable of love," I poked facetiously. He didn't smile; he was completely serious.

"You of all people should understand this," he said. "You've lost so many people that you've loved. Imagine going through

97

that again and again, lifetime after lifetime. Love is pain. Just imagine falling in love and having a family, a spouse and children. As an immortal you must watch as they all grow older and die, every one of them; watching your wife die, your children, and your grandchildren."

Bo was off in another world. He was staring at the ceiling wistfully. This wasn't a general warning, this was a memory.

"Oh Bo, is that why you left Lithuania? You had a family once?"

It's funny how sometimes you find out one little piece of information about someone, and suddenly so many things about them make sense. "Is that why you went back also?"

"You should see my great great granddaughter, Em, she's beautiful."

"Oh Bo," I said and hugged him tightly. He shrugged me away and got out of bed. One small glimpse of the man behind the cold exterior was all he would allow.

"Come on," he said. "We have things to do. Lesson two is disease detection." Lesson two was going to have to wait. I wanted to go home first; I wanted some of my own clothes! For now, it was sweatpants and a sweater of Bo's, both too big but it was better than that slinky black dress I'd been wearing. I felt bad that René wasn't going to get her dress back, but she said she was going on a shopping spree soon, she could replace it.

Upstairs Brian and Li were waiting for us. Li hugged me and then pulled back, eyeing me carefully. He put his hands on the sides of my face and pulled up my top lip with his thumbs revealing my fangs and sighed.

"It's okay, Umpa," I said using Wu's name for his grandfather. "Wu saved me."

Tears welled up in Li's eyes. "How is he?" The old man's voice cracked.

"He's good. They did turn him, Umpa." I hated telling him that but he needed to know, and he had assumed that already, I'm sure.

"But he's good. They treat him well, but they don't want him to leave, and we're trying to figure out why."

We all went up to Bo's office to sit down and talk. I got lightheaded walking up the stairs, and Bo noticed my unsteadiness. He took my arm and led me to the couch.

"You need to eat, Em! You have to hunt."

The thought of biting into a person or animal and completely draining its blood until it was dead still bothered me.

"I don't want to kill, Bo, isn't there another way?"

Brian, who had sat down beside me, pushed up his sleeve and stuck his arm out in front of me.

"No!" Bo said. "She needs to learn to hunt for herself. You won't always be here for her."

"She doesn't want to, and I will always be here for Em."

"Oh really," Bo asked. "Where will you be in eighty years, because she'll be right here with me, still needing to learn how to hunt for herself."

"Dude, why you gotta be such a…"

I bit into Brian's arm; I knew that was the best way of ending that statement and this argument. The warm blood filled my mouth, and the sensation of warmth and power enveloped me.

"That's enough, Em," Bo said.

Oh, but I had just started. Reluctantly I pulled away and licked the wound so it would heal quickly. I looked up at Brian to make sure he was alright. He nodded.

"I'll always be here for you Em," he said putting his arm around me. "As long as I live," he added glaring at Bo.

"I know, Bri," I said and put my head on his shoulder.

I went on to tell the story of the mansion, again leaving out the real reason why I went there and the part where Wu and I pretended to have sex repeatedly. I told them about the people there and what I'd seen going on in the basement.

"Don't y'all have like a queen or somebody you can report this guy to," Brian suggested.

"You watch too many movies," Bo said pacing the office. "Vampires answer to no one. We have our stratum of importance: Antecedents, Ectypes, Seeds, aged respectively but we answer to no one man or woman."

"There is one you could go to for answers," Li suggested.

"Angelus?" Bo asked looking like he didn't like that idea at all.

"Who's Angelus?" I asked looking back and forth between Bo and Li.

"Angelus Beledonte," Li said. "The oldest living vampire in the world. Many go to him for his council."

"But..." Bo interrupted "...even if we find out what Arlo is hiding and why he doesn't want Wu to leave and what Li has to do with all this, then what? Wu promised not to leave if Arlo let the two of us go, Em, remember? Even if we find out everything, how are we going to get word to Wu? How are we going to get him out? I don't think Arlo is just going to let him walk out the front door especially if we find out what he's hiding. Wu doesn't even know if you're still alive!"

Bo was always the pessimist, but he had a point. There was no way for us to get back into the mansion. We had no way to communicate with Wu. No contact with anyone on the inside.

"Wait a minute! What if I knew a way we could get in touch with Wu?"

"How?" Bo asked.

"I befriended a girl while I was there. What if I knew where she was going to be on what day? I could give her a message to give to Wu!"

"How would you know that?" Bo asked.

"She told me her birthday was the 27th and she always goes on a shopping spree at a mall downtown for her birthday. She said her boyfriend takes her every year, and he's a vamp so it would have to be at night!"

Bo paced back and forth across the office a few times.

"How much do you trust this girl?" he asked

"Moderately," I answered.

"We wouldn't have time to go see Angelus and get back before then, but we can at least let him know you're alright and that we're trying to figure things out."

Bo was still pacing back and forth. Li was sitting there as silent as ever, and Brian was sipping a cup of coffee. Oh coffee, I missed coffee! I took the cup from Brian's hand and removed the lid and took a big whiff. It still smelled like coffee.

"Don't do it, Em," Bo warned from across the room.

One tiny little sip wouldn't hurt, just one tiny drink. I tipped up the cup and took a mouthful of warm liquid. I expected the familiar robust flavor of strongly brewed gas station coffee, but it tasted nothing like that. It was horrible and bitter. I took one more drink just to make sure. Yes, it smelled the same but tasted nothing like coffee.

"You really shouldn't have done that, Em. Go to the bathroom," Bo said.

"Why?"

"You'll see." He smirked in an 'I told you so' kind of way.

In just a minute I knew why. It wasn't the same whole body nauseous feeling that I was used to, but it felt the same in my stomach. That knotted gross feeling before you throw up. I got up and quickly ran downstairs to the shop's bathroom. When I stood up from the toilet Bo was standing there holding out a paper towel to me.

"See, I told you. Em, you do know that I've been a vampire for nearly three hundred years, I might know what I'm talking about on the subject."

"I just wanted to see what it tasted like."

"Yes, but now you've wasted all the blood you took in, and it's like you haven't fed at all. Your friend's devotion was for naught."

Bo sighed loudly.

"You're going to be a pain in the neck to train aren't you?" he said.

"Seems fitting." I smiled "Since you're no longer a pain in mine," I said spitefully.

"Come on," he said. We've got work to do."

Back upstairs we were making plans, and I felt like I was in a spy movie. Brian was sitting at Bo's desk on the computer looking up the malls near the mansion because I couldn't remember the name of the one René had said.

"I think you and Brian should go into the mall together. You'll be less conspicuous as a couple walking around," Bo advised. "You may want to change up your look a bit, Em, in case the boyfriend might recognize you, a hat, something. If need be, Brian can distract him so you can talk to the girl if the opportunity doesn't come up on its own."

"I don't know what to say to her, what message do we want to send to Wu?" I asked.

"You should write a note," Brian suggested. "It's more personal and tangible. Words can be twisted around; a note will say exactly what you want it to.

"Perfect," Bo said,

Holy cow, did the two of them just agree on something?

Li grabbed a piece of paper; we knew Wu would recognize his grandfather's handwriting.

"I think we should keep it fairly cryptic just in case," Bo said.

"I know!" I said. "Tell him I'm looking into the problem with the laundry."

Li also put something in there about hungry ghosts. He said it had something to do with Halloween traditions. Wu would expect to hear something from us by Halloween.

"Okay, so we'll have a little over a month to go to Bulgaria, find out what Arlo is hiding, and come up with a plan to get Wu out of the heavily guarded mansion, piece of cake," Bo said.

"Whoa wait, Bulgaria?!" I asked.

"Yeah," Bo answered. "Did you think the oldest living vampire in the world would live here in the U.S.? Grab your passport; it's going to be a long trip."

"I don't have a passport; I don't even have my driver's license, remember! So, I don't know how I can even get a passport now, and it's not like the DMV is open at midnight," I whined.

"Don't worry; there are ways vampires can acquire such documents. I'll take care of it. For now, we have some training to do."

ELEVEN

We had to go to my house before I started Bo's "training". I wanted to be in my own clothes and get some shoes for crying out loud. I'd been without shoes since my first day at the mansion. I wanted to see Bacon too; I missed his sweet, little furry face. As soon as I got to my house, I yelled for him, and he came running down the stairs and jumped into my arms but immediately jumped back out and whimpered. I thought maybe he'd hurt himself jumping, but it only took a moment to realize that he knew I was different, and he didn't like it. Bo waited impatiently while I tried to convince Bacon that I was still me and wouldn't hurt him. It did take some time, but he eventually climbed onto my lap and laid down, but I could tell he was still on edge.

Bo hurried me out the door to start our disease detection lesson. We walked around for awhile, him asking me to smell the air every so often. I never could smell blood like I was supposed to, I smelled the surroundings more. Bo said acquiring the taste would better help me detect the scents, but I was still reluctant to kill no matter how hungry I was. Bo was becoming frustrated, I could tell. We walked around for a long time and I assumed he was looking for someone with a particular disease to see if I could smell it.

"Alright, let's try something else. I'm going to go this way, and you go that way. I want you to use your sense of smell and see when you can detect me since you already know my scent, okay?"

"Okay," I said, then walked off down the alley that he'd pointed to. At the end of the alley, I wasn't sure which direction I should go. I wandered aimlessly, sniffing the air every few seconds to see if I could smell anything different. I did detect something in the air, but I didn't know what it was.

"Hey there, sweetheart, are you lost?" a scruffy creepy man asked me.

"No, I'm meeting a friend," I answered curtly.

"I'll be your friend, baby."

"No, you'll go away and leave me the hell alone," I said without fear. The old me, the mortal me, may have been scared, but this me wasn't at all.

"Oh come on, don't be like that, baby," he said and grabbed my arm. I pulled loose, but he grabbed me again.

"You're a frisky one; I like em frisky."

Okay, time for some superhuman vampire strength. I fought against him. I hit him, I pushed, I shoved. My fighting against him always broke his grip, but he kept coming back, and I was getting tired. I didn't think vampires got tired like this. I was weak, and I was dizzy. Oh no, if I pass out it's hard to tell what he'll do to me. I tried yelling for Bo, but the man put his hand over my mouth. That was a very bad decision on his part.

I turned my head to the right and bit down on the man's wrist and took long draws of blood. Surely it wouldn't take much to incapacitate him. He finally went limp and fell to the ground, but I held on to his wrist drinking, much longer than I had with Brian. I felt so energized, so much stronger, more awake, more alive. I could feel the warmth coursing through my veins. I heard someone coming, oh no! I didn't know what to do. I panicked for just a second until I heard Bo's voice.

"It's me," he announced.

"Bo, I didn't...he attacked me...I didn't mean..."

"Shhh, Em, it's okay. You did what you had to do."

"Is he going to live?" I asked.

Bo bent down and touched his arm. I wasn't sure if he was feeling for a pulse or if he had some other vampire way of telling how much blood was left by the feel of his skin.

"No, he's too far gone," he said and bit into his other wrist taking the last of his blood.

"I didn't want to do this, Bo, I didn't want to," I said pacing back and forth.

"Em, you're a vampire now. This is how you eat. You have to kill."

"But I don't want to; I don't want to kill in order to eat."

"Seriously, Em, where do you think hamburger and steak come from? Thousands of animals are slaughtered every day to feed people, what's the difference?"

I hadn't thought about it that way. I guess it was the same concept, but I was doing the killing instead of somebody else. I hadn't just eaten an animal, though, this was a human.

"How did he taste to you?" Bo asked.

"I don't know, kind of bitter, a little like motor oil."

"That was on his hands. He must have been some kind of mechanic, what else? How was it different from Brian's blood?"

"Brian's blood seemed warmer, thicker, and Brian's blood kind of has a hum to it, does that makes sense?"

"Yes," Bo answered. "That's the nicotine in his blood. This man wasn't a smoker. Can you detect that aftertaste?" Bo asked smacking his lips together.

"Yeah, I think so."

"This man had a very poor diet; I'd say lots of fast food, greasy hamburgers and such."

"So what do we do now?" I asked looking down at the man's body.

"Come on, we'll throw him in the Holston River, it's not far."

Bo threw the man over his shoulder, and we cautiously made our way to the riverbank. I felt bad when he tossed the man into the water, and I wondered for a moment if he had a family.

Bo and I walked in silence for awhile and when two teenage boys walked by I sniffed the air.

"What?" Bo asked, "What do you smell?"

"They smell like Brian tastes. Nicotine? Those boys smoke, too."

"Yes! Bo said sounding proud of my observation. "There's hope for you yet," he teased.

"Bo, what did I taste like?"

"You tasted like a spice that I couldn't place, something that I've long forgotten, something Italian perhaps." He smiled at the memory.

"Will I not taste like that now?" I asked.

"You would taste somewhat the same but not quite since your diet is different now. You will see that everyone and everything tastes just a little different, it all has its own distinction. It wouldn't have the warmth it once had either."

"So we can drink vampire blood, it's just not warm?"

Bo didn't answer, but stopped walking and pulled me to him and leaned his head to one side. He was inviting me to taste him. I ran my face up his neck taking in his scent first. It seemed incredibly erotic that I was going to bite him on the neck right here in the middle of the dark street. I opened my mouth and placed it on his skin and very gently bit into him. After just a second I pulled back and shivered, the moment completely ruined.

"I see what you mean."

It wasn't an enjoyable experience at all. It was a little like taking a bite of cold soup. His blood wasn't actually cold, but it wasn't warm and inviting like it was supposed to be. I thought about Brian's blood and my mouth watered. I longed for my friend's hot thick blood that electrified my body.

Bo said we'd had enough for tonight, and we made our way back home. I wasn't the slightest bit tired even though it was almost dawn. I was full of energy from the blood I'd taken. Bo went to bed, and I stayed up watching TV. I sat there thinking about that man I killed wondering if I should feel guilty or not. I didn't attack him, he attacked me, so which one of us was really the monster? I decided I wasn't going to feel guilty. If he hadn't attacked me, it could have been someone else, someone incapable of defending themselves. I found much solace in that.

I was awoken by Bo rudely plopping down on the couch. I pulled my feet from behind his back and sat up.

"What time is it?" I asked.

"Eight," he said pulling his sleeve back to check his watch. He was already dressed in a green and black flannel shirt and his usual black pants.

"I suppose you're wanting to start training already?" I said rubbing my eyes. Why, oh why, could vampires not drink coffee?

"Not particularly," he answered. "We got a lot in last night."

I looked at him dubiously, my training last night was a total failure.

"Last night was a disaster, Bo."

"Was it? You detected nicotine in that kid's scent. You learned how weak you become if you don't feed and how dangerous that can be, and you made your first kill. I'd say my lessons were fairly successful last night," he said smugly.

I don't know how he could be so smug. It's not like he made all that happen, it was just chance...wasn't it? Wait, was it? Did Bo set me up? Were we walking around all that time looking for a particular scent, or was he looking for a shady situation to lure me into? Did he bait me out to that guy to get me to kill him?

"Bo, did you set me up last night?"

He didn't answer; he just sat there with that smug look on his face.

"Did. You. Set. Me. Up? I repeated angrily.

"Don't get your panties in a bunch, Em, it's a proven training method. It's just like a parent letting go of a bike when teaching their child how to ride."

"It is NOT! I killed a man, Bo; I killed a man because of you!" I yelled at him.

"I don't know what you're getting so upset about. It's not like I made that guy attack you. That was his choice," Bo yelled back.

We were both standing now and screaming at each other.

"You knowingly led me into danger!"

"I knew you could handle it, and if not I was right there if I needed to jump in."

With that I lunged at Bo, my hands going for his throat.

TWELVE

He grabbed both of my arms and twisted me around so that my back was against him and my arms were crossed in front of my chest.

"Lesson three, just because you're a vampire doesn't mean you can fight any better."

He kissed me on the cheek. "Experience always wins," he said and pushed me away from him. I lunged at him again, and he quickly spun me around and whispered in my ear.

"You can't beat me, Em."

His playfulness only made me even angrier.

"You'd be better off fighting Brian, let him go, Li."

I looked to the top of the stairs, and Li was standing in front of Brian who looked both mad and concerned. They must have heard us yelling and came to check on us.

Brian came down the stairs. "I'd much rather fight you," he said glaring at Bo.

"Come now, Brian, we all know you're going to step up and do exactly what Em needs…"

I wasn't sure what exactly he meant by that. I didn't know whether it was meant to be a compliment or an insult.

"…and right now she needs to know the extent of her limits."

Bo dug into the pocket of his pants and held up a bill.

"Fifty bucks to the first one to pin the other."

Brian turned toward me. "I'm game if you are, Em, but I don't want to hurt you."

"Who says you're going to hurt me?" I sneered, still aggravated from my encounter with Bo.

"Alright," Brian said taking off his outer shirt.

I lunged at him, and he evaded my grasp. We went round and round, back and forth. I could see what Bo meant about experience being better than strength. I'd never been in a fight in my whole life; I knew Brian had been in several. I was fast, and I was strong, but that didn't compare to an experienced fighter. Being a vampire wasn't exactly what I thought it would be. It seemed more like a weakness than a superpower sometimes. There were all these things I had to avoid, and only a few things were better. I had a feeling Brian was taking it easy on me, so I made sure he knew that I wasn't holding back. I actually got him to the ground a couple times but couldn't pin him down. I did manage to rip his shirt off, and I felt bad. It was his white shirt with gray skulls all over it, and I knew it was one of his favorites. We fought and wrestled for awhile, and I admired Brian's persistence. He was probably just doing it for the money. I wasn't sure how long ago he'd lost his job, and I knew money was tight for him. I was too much in my own head at the moment, and Brian got the drop on me; I may have been able to get away, but I didn't try. He pinned me to the ground and smiled. He helped me up then walked over to Bo to collect his reward.

"Sorry about your shirt, I know it was one of your favorites. I'll buy you another one," I said.

"Oh yeah," he exclaimed. "Fifty bucks and a new shirt!"

Bo and I left to continue our lessons, and I was dreading them and whatever kind of trickery he had up his sleeve tonight. He may have gotten me to kill, but now I didn't trust him as far as I could throw him.

"Well since you're not going to eat a human or something as easy as a dog, and trust me, you don't even want to try to sink your teeth into a cat...tell me, Em, what would you eat?"

I thought about that for a moment.

"What about a rat or a guinea pig or something?"

"Too little blood, you need something bigger," Bo replied.

"A rabbit," I suggested.

"Yeah, I'm sure we can find something along those lines. Okay, let's go hunting."

"Hunting? We can't just go down to the pet store?" I asked.

"That'll get expensive, Em, you'll need at least two or three of something that small a night."

"Do I have to kill absolutely every night?" I whined.

"Yes, Em, you have to eat! You ate every day as a mortal, and you have to eat every day as a vampire. If you hadn't been starving yourself the last few days, Brian wouldn't have beaten you today."

"I let him win," I said defensively.

"Yeah, okay," Bo said sarcastically.

"Well not at first, but I got to thinking about how he probably really needed the money now that he lost his job, and I admit Brian did out maneuver me, but once he got me down I let him pin me."

Bo didn't say anything more on that subject. We walked to the edge of town, I hadn't realized how much traveling Bo did on foot, but I didn't get tired. Once we were in the woods Bo had me close my eyes and listen. I heard the rustling of leaves, and we slowly and quietly headed in that direction. I hadn't realized it before, but here away from all the street lights, it was easy to see in the dark. We did see a few squirrels, but

Bo said they were too small to deal with. Eventually, we did walk up on a rabbit.

"Well, what are you waiting for? Go get him," Bo said.

I took off running, and so did the rabbit. I was much faster as a vampire than I was as a mortal, but the rabbit changed directions so quickly. I slid on the fallen leaves, and Bo laughed hysterically with each fall I took. I had never seen Bo laugh so much, and it irritated me. I finally gave up.

"What am I doing wrong?" I huffed.

"Nothing," Bo said. "Like anything it just takes practice. Let's find you some slower prey, hmm."

We walked further into the woods and finally came upon a raccoon who didn't seem alarmed at our presence.

"Will you eat that?" Bo whispered.

I nodded, and Bo pushed me forward. I walked toward it, and it didn't start to run until I was very close. I grabbed him and picked him up.

"You need to bite him, Em, quickly!"

I looked back at Bo and in that moment of hesitation the raccoon bit me, and I

123

almost dropped him. I sunk my teeth into his back and drank until he was empty.

"Lesson number four," Bo said as I walked back to him. "Wild animals bite."

"Yeah thanks, I got it."

"Describe the taste," Bo said to me.

I thought about it briefly. It was really hard to put the taste into words because it wasn't sour or sweet or tangy. It was like trying to describe different kinds of red wine. It was all wine, but the flavors were slightly different.

"I don't know, it tasted kind of...wild, I guess. Like the way the forest smells, the leaves, the river...just...wild."

"Excellent," he said to me. "Now what blood have you found preferable?"

"Well, I like the raccoon better than that guy last night. He didn't taste very good to me, kind of bitter and greasy, but Brian's blood has been by far the best."

I thought about how badly I desired my best friend's blood, and it bothered me.

"What's the best thing you've ever tasted?" I asked Bo.

"Humans of an earlier time," he responded. "Around the 19th century, I believe. Advanced medicine was widespread, and you didn't have to worry about disease as much. It was before all the processed food and preservatives of today. You can still find blood like that these days, but it's very rare. There is a certain diet that some follow where they only eat real food, Paleo I think it's called. Their blood tastes amazing, Em. You must try it some time."

We wandered the woods talking and hunting. Bo taught me a lot about hunting that night, catching a few other critters. He always had me compare the tastes of things. We headed back home well before dawn. Bo was terrified of the sun, and I can't say I could blame him. Bursting into flames seemed like a horrible way to die. I was glad I'd spent a few days at the mansion in the sunroom and outside with René. I was able to say goodbye to the sun. Not that I was ever much of a daytime person anyway. Bo went to bed, and I slept on the couch again mainly because I was still mad at him for leading me into danger so I would kill that man. I understood his motives, but I was still mad.

When I woke up, Bo was gone so I went upstairs to see if anyone was here.

The shop was dark, but the light was on in Bo's office. Brian greeted me from behind Bo's desk. He was the only one in the room.

"Well there you are, sleepy head," he said.

I looked at the clock on the wall it was 10:30, I had slept late. I guess a night of chasing down forest animals had tired me out.

"I don't think Bo would be too happy about you sitting at his desk, Bri."

"Actually he told me to. I'm looking into flights to Bulgaria."

"Why? I mean, why are you doing it?"

"Haven't you heard? I'm on the payroll now. I'm the new day man," he said proudly.

I stood there in shock for a minute. Had Bo just done something nice for Brian? I'd mentioned about him being hard up for money the day before, and then Bo offered him a job.

"Hey, Bo said he'd be out for awhile, you want to go catch a midnight movie?"

I thought about that. It would be nice to watch a movie like we used to. I thought about sitting next to him in the theater, and it made me want his blood. The thought disturbed me. I knew I wouldn't kill my friend, that's not what bothered me, just how badly I wanted to bite him. What if I took too much blood one day? I never wanted to do anything to hurt Brian.

"Are you okay, Em? You don't look so hot."

"Gee thanks," I said.

"You just look a little pale I guess."

"He said to the vampire," I joked.

"You need a snack, babe?" he asked holding up his arm.

I did! I really wanted his blood, but would I be able to stop without Bo being here to tell me when?

THIRTEEN

"No! I mean…umm, no, I'm good, thanks. I just have to run out real quick. I can meet you there at the theater if that's cool."

"It's a date," he said and went back to what he was doing. Okay, I had about an hour to hunt. I needed enough blood to ensure Brian's safety at the movies. I hurried to the edge of town and entered the woods. I was going to kill the first thing I came to, no question, no hesitation. Okay, so maybe not the first thing I came to because it was an opossum. Bo said they were almost as evil as cats and tasted like garbage. The very next thing, though. I stood there behind a large tree with my eyes closed listening to the night. I heard something coming. I didn't recognize the scent so it must be something I hadn't eaten, which could be anything since I'd only had raccoon and fox thus far.

I stood there waiting in the dark. I could see fairly well, though. Holy crap, it was a deer! Could I take down a deer? Bo said he'd taken down a mountain lion before, but he knew what he was doing. I guess it wouldn't hurt to try, what's the worst that could happen? It's not like it could kill me. Deer were fairly peaceful animals, right? I'd watched Bambi. This definitely wasn't Bambi, though, maybe him all grown up. It had antlers. I was a little leery, but if I could catch him, I could leave already and have more time to get ready instead of trying to catch two or three small critters. I was going to go for it. I quietly waited for him to get closer. He stopped a couple times to sniff the air but kept coming closer, and then I attacked.

I must have totally scared the bejesus out of him because he did this crazy back bending twist thing in the air that totally caught me off guard, hooves were flying at my face. Had he not done that, I would've had a hold on him already, but he took off running, and so did I. He was fast, but I was able to keep up. I planned to make a leap for it and grab his antlers; that seemed sensible to me, but just as I made my jump he changed directions. I only landed one hand on his small horns, and one of the two points jammed into my hand. This sent a surge of adrenaline through my body. He was still in motion dragging me beside him across the ground. I reached over and grabbed his other horn, and with a determined scream, I twisted his head around. He lost his balance and came tumbling over on top of me. Geez, this sucker was heavy. Before he could get up again, I bit into his neck.

I didn't get a good bite, and blood sprayed all over my face and shirt. Great! He was a lot to drink, almost as much as a human, I'd wager. He had a nutty gamey kind of taste that I didn't particularly care for, but it wasn't bad. I drank him all and pushed his heavy body off of mine. I was pretty proud of myself for taking down such a large and fast animal. Of course, Bo wasn't here to see it. I would definitely tell him about my accomplishment later. It probably didn't look nearly as cool in real life as I imagine it did in my head. I think I looked a lot like those cowboys that steer wrestle or whatever it's called, grabbing the animal by the horns and digging my heels into the ground. Yeah, it was probably a good thing Bo wasn't here to ruin it for me because I'm sure it was much more glamorous in my head.

I headed back to the shop. I'd wash up there then go to my house to get ready. I can imagine the reaction if someone saw me right now, covered in blood. When I got there, I realized I didn't have a vehicle. Mine had been left at the mansion, Bo was still out, and Brian was already gone. I wouldn't be able to go to my house across town and make it to the movies in time. As it was, I barely had enough time to walk to the theater. I hurried downstairs to shower. I was glad I had grabbed some clothes last time I was at my house. I'd grabbed clothes but not any extra shoes. Oh boy, I hope the fashion police weren't going to be at the theater. I really needed my tall black boots with this outfit, but my pink and gray tennis shoes would have to do.

I checked my watch; I had twenty minutes to get there. I would have to run; maybe my tennis shoes were a good thing.

Outside I took off in the direction of the theater. It actually felt good to run. I hated running as a mortal, mostly because it made my legs hurt and I would always get that pain in the side of my stomach, but this felt good. I didn't feel any pain at all, and the wind in my face felt nice. I felt wild and free. I sped up just to see how fast I could go. I was fast, really fast. I mean, I wasn't the Flash or anything; I couldn't outrun a car, but maybe somebody on a bike or something. I got to the theater right on time. I wasn't tired at all, and I was just barely winded. I was glad Brian hadn't wanted to go to our usual theater; it would've taken me over an hour to get there on foot.

"There you are," Brian said. "I was starting to wonder if you were going to show."

"Sorry, I would've texted but you know my phone is gone, I left my purse in my car at the mansion. Ah, crap!"

I just realized I hadn't brought a purse or wallet with me. I had no money.

"I got ya covered, babe," Brian said realizing what I'd forgotten. "I just got a new job, ya know. My boss is a total douche bag, but he did front me my first paycheck."

Brian smiled as he pulled out some cash and bought our tickets. The movie was too loud for my heightened hearing, but it felt nice to do something normal.

After the movie, I stepped outside and took a deep breath, and I caught something familiar. I sniffed the air a couple more times.

"What is it?" Brian asked.

"Bo is here." I walked toward his scent. "Bo," I called out.

He stepped out from the shadows and smiled.

"Very good, Em," he commended.

"How did you know we were here?" Brian asked Bo. "You were gone when we left."

"I followed Em's scent. I know her scent better than anyone else's; it was easy to follow since she walked here."

"Oh Em, I didn't know that. I would've waited for you," Brian said.

"No, it's okay, I really enjoyed running here."

Brian's mouth dropped open in over-exaggerated shock.

"Oh shut up," I laughed and pushed him.

"I'll take you back to the shop," Brian offered. "Bo, do you need a ride?"

Wow, there was hope for the two of these guys to get along yet!

"No, I came to take Em hunting," Bo said.

"I already went," I stated proudly like a kid that had poured their own cereal for the first time. "So I will take that ride. I need to swing by my place first and pick up some clothes, if that's okay?"

Bo went hunting, and Brian and I went to my place. Upstairs Brian sat on my bed while I dug out clothes and stuffed them into a duffle bag. I sat down next to him and fell backward on my bed.

"Ahhh, I miss my bed! I miss my room and my house. I wish I could stay here."

"Why can't you?" Brian asked, and I just shot him a look.

"You know I can't sleep here in the day time."

"It's just because of the sunlight, right? There is no rule that you have to sleep underground is there?" he asked.

"Right," I answered.

"There's only this one window in here, I can fix it to where no sunlight comes in. You could sleep in your bed tonight if you wanted."

"Really?"

"Yeah, there's still that big piece of plywood downstairs that we were going to cover your living room window with when it was broken last year, but you had it fixed so fast we didn't use it. I'm going to need the real story on what happened there now, by the way."

Brian hung cardboard over my window and taped it in place then I helped hold the plywood while he screwed it to the wall. Just for good measure and appearance purposes we also hung a dark blanket over the plywood. I told him the real story of how my living room window had been broken and the crazy vampire battle in my living room while we worked. Brian also put cardboard over the window at the end of the hallway outside my bedroom. He stayed up all night to make sure my room was sunlight proof. We were both exhausted.

"You can go ahead and sleep, Em, I'll stay up and make sure all the sunlight is blacked out."

"Thanks, Bri, you're the best."

"I can't be. You currently hold that position," he replied.

I fell asleep knowing I was in good hands under the watch of my best friend.

FOURTEEN

"I was so worried when I woke up and you weren't there."

I opened my eyes to see Bo sitting there on my bed staring at me.

"Why didn't you come home, Em, are you angry with me?"

"No," I said trying to comprehend such a serious discussion so soon after waking up.

"Why didn't you come home?" he repeated.

"I am home Bo, this is my home."

"Not anymore, you're a vampire now. You need to stay with me. This place isn't safe enough."

"We blacked out the window, double layered it. We even covered the one in the hallway. Sunlight can't get through."

"What about Arlo, what if he sent someone after you? You're unprotected here," Bo argued.

"That's absurd, Arlo doesn't even know that I'm still alive, Bo."

"Well, what if I just want you there, what if I need you by my side and I'm out of excuses?" he said seriously.

"Oh, Bo." I sat up and hugged him, and he hugged me back tightly. His divulgences of emotions were so few and far between I almost felt guilty hearing them, like they were a secret that no person was meant to hear. He laid me back on the bed and began kissing my lips and neck, kissing me like he did when I was a mortal.

Bo kissed me repeatedly; it felt familiar, and it was nice. It also had a lingering feeling of heartbreak. It was subtle, like a shadow or a memory. I let him hold me, hug me, and caress my body, and I wanted more.

"Make love to me, Bo," I requested.

"I can't, I can't bite you now, vampire blood doesn't work. I'm sorry Em… unbelievably sorry," he joked.

He kissed me a few more times then laid next to me with his arms around me.

"I don't like you not coming home, even if you just sleep on the couch. I need to know you're safe."

I had so enjoyed sleeping in my own house and in my own bed, but I wasn't going to argue the point now.

"Come on," he said. "Let's go hunting."

"Where's Brian?" I asked.

"I sent him on some errands. We need to prepare for your meeting with René tomorrow night."

I got up, and Bo watched me intently while I changed clothes. It was a much shorter walk to the woods from my house than it was from the shop. I told Bo about my victorious hunting trip the night before in great detail, and he said he was proud of me. Bo caught the scent of a mountain lion and had me hang back and watch him. He moved quietly and steadily as he stalked his prey. I stood there and admired the way he moved. Each step was calculated, each movement precise. Bo took off running, and I kept pace behind him. I hadn't even seen the large cat when Bo pounced, but I stopped and stood back for him to make the kill like he'd instructed me to do. After just a second he motioned for me to join him. I liked mountain lion, it was the best thing I'd tasted so far, aside from Brian, of course. It was enough that Bo and I were content but not full.

As soon as we drank her, Bo pounced again, and it took me off guard because this time, he pounced on me. He picked me up and pinned me against a tree and proceeded to fulfill my earlier request, well…with as much 'love' as was expected from Bo. With him, it was much more savage, even more so in the middle of the woods. It was primal. The experience was different now that I was a vampire. It was an odd combination, decreased sensations yet heightened awareness. It was still pleasurable but definitely different. We walked back to my place, then took his car back to the shop where Brian was waiting for us to go over the plans for tomorrow.

Bo sat on the couch next to me instead of pacing the room as usual. He put his arm around me, which was definitely out of character. Bo wasn't much for affection at all, let alone public affection. We went over what seemed like every possible scenario for tomorrow. I think we covered every "what if" in the world: what if it was more than just René and Bobby there, what if Bobby attacked me or Brian, what if we were attacked once outside the mall...etc. We went over what each of us would do in every situation. Our main plan was for me to catch René alone in one of the shops and for Brian to distract Bobby if need be. Bo was going to hang back but stay close enough that if there was any trouble he could help. We were already taking a chance that Bobby would recognize me. Bo even had Brian pull up a map of the mall so we could go over where Bo planned on being and what route we should take in and out of the mall. It felt like a military grade operation.

Our planning consumed most of the night. When we were done, Brian offered to drive me home.

"No!" Bo said as soon as he offered. "She's staying here with me. Isn't that right?" Bo asked holding out his hand to help me up off the couch.

"Ah...yeah, sure." He was acting really weird, even for Bo.

"How about another hunting trip?" he asked kissing my hand. He hadn't done that since the night he'd pretended to be my boyfriend at the club last year.

"Umm...yeah sure, I'll be down in a minute."

Bo hesitated for a moment then walked out of the office and downstairs.

"Okay, what's up with Bo?" I asked Brian wondering if he knew something I didn't. "He's acting really strange."

"He's marking his territory, Em," Brian said.

"Huh?"

"He's jealous. I'm pretty sure he thinks we slept together last night."

"But Bo doesn't get jealous, well...he says he doesn't."

I'd thought Bo was jealous a few times myself, but he always got mad and adamantly denied it.

"Wow, even with undead super powers you're still clueless, Em."

"Hey! I'm not dead...or undead, whatever that even means." I never understood that term. If you were undead didn't that mean you were alive? Why did they use that term to describe vampires and zombies?

"Yep, totally undead; you were dead, Arlo killed you, then Jet Li brought you back...therefore...undead."

Well, I guess if you put it that way, it did make sense.

I met Bo downstairs for another hunting trip. I knew we weren't going to have any time to hunt in the morning. We were pressed for time as it was. We planned to leave at sunset; it was a three-hour drive. Luckily the mall was open later on Saturdays, but we were taking a chance of missing René and Bobby all together. Brian had suggested that we drive to North Carolina tonight and find a place to hideout until nightfall, but of course, Bo shot that idea down immediately.

Once outside and into the woods I bragged a bit about how fast I ran to the movie theater, and Bo challenged me to a race. We ran swiftly through the woods dodging trees, downed logs, and rocks, but it wasn't until the forest gave way to rolling hills that we were able to really open up. Bo, of course, was faster than me; he maneuvered easily through the obstacles in the forest not slowing much. I was more cautious. I was able to keep up with him outside of the forest, though. I was amazed at how good it felt to run. My muscles didn't ache, and my lungs didn't burn. I imagined this must be what it felt like to ride a motorcycle. Bo didn't slow down as we approached a wooden fence; he leapt easily over top of it. It was too late for me to slow down because I was going too fast. I made the leap but my feet caught the top of the fence, and I landed face-first on the ground.

Bo must have stopped not far ahead because I heard him laughing, and it annoyed me. I got up brushing the dirt from my clothes.

"It's all about the timing, Em, if you had jumped just a second earlier you would have cleared it."

He tried wiping something from my face, and I smacked his hand away still annoyed that he laughed at me. He laughed again and continued to wipe the dirt from my cheek.

"Dinner?" he said pointing down the field to a flock of sheep. I thought for a second about cute little fluffy white lambs, and the thought of blood splattered across their white coats made me cringe. Bo must have seen the expression on my face.

"Okay, no lamb chops. Can I interest you in a nice juicy steak, rare of course," he said pointing up the hill. I didn't see any cows, but I guessed Bo could smell them. I nodded.

Up the hill and across another fence we had our pick of a herd of cows. It was so easy, they didn't run from you, they didn't claw, scratch, or bite. I was able to walk right up to one, stroke its fir a few times, and it only flinched a little when I bit into its shoulder. It was easy food. I wondered why Bo didn't choose cows all the time. He said he didn't care for the taste much. The best part about cows was that I could drink a bit from a couple of them and not kill them. They weren't the best thing I'd tasted, but they weren't bad and were definitely the easiest. The convenience and not having to kill in order to eat had put cows at the top of my preferred food list.

Once we were done eating, Bo once again pounced on me pinning me to the ground. The old me, the mortal me, would have never gotten half naked out in the middle of an open field. In the woods it had been different; we were still concealed, hidden by the trees and brush. This field was vast and open. But this me, the vampire me, didn't really care. We lay there on our backs afterward looking up at the stars. It was one of the few times Bo stuck around after being intimate, and I liked that.

"Bo?"

"Hmm?"

"Brian and I are just friends; that's all we've ever been."

"Really, Em, I don't..."

I reached over and pinched his lips together.

"Shhhh, don't ruin it," I scolded. Something else I wouldn't have had the gumption to do as a mortal. I removed my hand.

"Okay, but I..."

I smacked my hand over top of his mouth again and left it there for a minute. He must have gotten the hint because he was silent when I finally removed it until he finally said it was time for us to get back. We had an important day tomorrow.

Bo drove quickly across the I-26. Much faster than the legal limit. Time wasn't on our side. I wondered what he would do if we got pulled over, did Bo even have a driver's license? I sat there in the passenger seat fiddling with the handle of a shopping bag. I had René's black lace dress dry cleaned and was bringing it back to her as a gift of good faith. If she wasn't willing to give Wu our note maybe the gesture would persuade her. During the drive, we went over our plan of action again, and it made me a little nervous. No doubt if I was still mortal I'd be losing my mind right now. We made good time until we got into the city. Bo had gotten us there in two hours, but traffic was slowing us down now. By the time we got to the mall, it was just two hours before closing.

As planned, Bo parked on the ground level of the mall parking garage. Brian and I would start our search there, and Bo would go in on the top level entrance. I made sure I had our letter to give René tucked into my back pocket. I wore jeans, a large frumpy tunic, and had my hair tucked into a big knit cap trying to look unrecognizable. Bo was also dressed in disguise. This was the first time I'd ever seen him wear jeans, and he looked amazing in them. He wore a t-shirt and a baseball hat, and it would be hard for even me to spot him looking like that.

"Well here goes nothing," I said to Brian as we walked in.

Bo and I both knew what René looked like, but Brian didn't. I told him he'd know her if he saw her.

"Okay, what does that mean?" he asked.

"Think Jessica Rabbit meets Marylyn Monroe."

He just whistled. We covered the entire first floor pretending to shop and were halfway through the second when Brian's phone rang. It was Bo from the third floor saying he thought he'd spotted them below on the second floor in front of the ice cream shop. Bo stayed on the phone till we got there, in case they started moving. We cautiously turned the corner, looked around, then I grabbed the phone from Brian.

"Seriously Bo, did you not see her that night. She was like the hottest girl ever, that's not her.

In front of us stood a girl with dark orange curly hair and freckles... nothing like René's crimson waves and milky skin.

"I'm sorry, I must have been distracted by trying to break you out of a house full of vampires," Bo said.

I was about to say something smart back to him, but just then I spotted Bobby leaned up against the banister outside of a store farther down.

"Bo, I found them."

"Where?" he asked.

"Bobby is outside of Deb holding a bunch of shopping bags. You see him?"

"Yep, be careful," he said and hung up.

Brian and I circled around so I could walk into the store with my back completely toward Bobby. I went into the

149

store alone, and Brian stayed outside to distract Bobby if need be, just as planned. I scanned the store for René and spotted her in the back with half a dozen things thrown over her arm, headed toward the dressing room. Here we go; my heart was actually beating at a normal pace instead of the slow thump I'd grown accustomed to as of late.

Just as she got to the dressing room, I pulled her black lace dress from my shopping bag.

"You really should try this one on," I said.

She looked at me and her mouth dropped open. This was the moment of truth. There really was no reason for her not to be happy to see me, but I didn't know what went on after I left the mansion or what Arlo said happened. He could've made me out to be public enemy number one. She stood there in shock as the seconds ticked by. Finally, she grabbed me and hugged me tightly.

"Lord alive, Emina, is it really you? I thought you were dead," she said in her thick Louisiana accent.

"Come on," I said peeking out the front of the store and pulling her into the dressing room and locking the door behind us.

"Arlo said you tried to trick him; he said he killed you."

"He did kill me," I answered and opened my mouth to show her my fangs. "Well, he tried."

She looked at me again in shock.

"How's Wu?" I asked.

"He's okay, I think. Arlo stuck him downstairs for awhile. There's all kinds of talk about you being some sort of spy and Wu being in on it. Nobody really knows what happened, but Arlo threw a hissy. He's been on the rampage, he just up and killed Jennifer one day, said he couldn't trust her. What really happened?"

"Can I trust you René?"

"Of course you can, sugah."

"I knew Wu before the mansion, we were friends. He was kidnapped and changed against his will. I came to try and rescue him."

She didn't say anything else but pondered that newfound truth.

"I need you to do something for me, René."

She set her stack of clothes on the bench in the dressing room.

"Go on," she said.

I pulled the envelope out of my back pocket and held it out to her.

"Can you give this to Wu?"

"Oh, Em, I don't know, Arlo is so suspicious right now. If he caught me giving Wu a letter, he would kill me. He really has lost it."

"Please. I just want to let him know I'm okay."

"Arlo will kill me if he catches me with it. Can I just give him a message?" she pleaded.

"Yes. That will work," I conceded. "I don't want you to put yourself in danger. It sounds like Arlo is pretty scary right now. Just tell him that I'm okay and that I'm going to figure this out."

"Oh, honey, you have no idea how scary he is right now. He trusts no one. All the girls are scared to death. I'm surprised he hasn't canceled the soiree next month, but I will give Wu your message, I promise."

Did she just seriously use the word soiree?

"Why are you having a party?" I asked.

"We have one every year; it's the 19th annual All Hallows Eve costume party. We've got to have a little fun some time." She smiled.

"A costume party?" I asked.

"Yes, of course, it's Halloween."

"Are there usually a lot of people there?" I asked.

"Yes, we usually have a good turnout."

"And security?"

"It's fairly relaxed I guess, the front door anyway. People come and go all evening."

I was forming a plan in my head.

"You're going to sneak in aren't you?" she asked.

"Maybe, I..."

We were interrupted by a knock on the dressing room door. My body went rigid.

"I'm sorry, ladies, you can't do this. Only one person to a dressing room please," a voice said, and I relaxed.

"Thank you, René," I said as I hugged her. Now I had to slip back out of the store without Bobby noticing me.

"Oh hey," she said as I slipped out the dressing room door. "I found your purse. It's in the car that we brought here."

"Where'd you park?" I asked.

"Level three," she answered.

"Thanks again," I said and made my way to the front of the store. The clerk who knocked on the door was eyeing me suspiciously like I was trying to steal something. I was really hoping she wouldn't make a scene. Brian saw me approaching the front of the store and stepped to the other side of Bobby and asked him something. Bobby looked down at his watch, and I took that opportunity to slip out of the store and walk quickly out of Bobby's line of sight.

Brian caught up to me and right on cue his cell phone rang. He handed it right to me, and I told Bo we were coming up then I handed it back to Brian. We made our way to the nearest escalator to the third floor where Bo was waiting at the top. I didn't stop there but kept walking quickly passed him.

"What happened, what's wrong?" Bo asked.

"Nothing's wrong. I need to get to the parking garage."

"Why? What happened?" Bo asked again.

"I need to get to my car before they do and get my stuff."

"So, did she take the letter? Is she going to help us?"

"No, but yes," I said as we walked quickly toward the exit door.

I could tell Bo was getting annoyed by my lack of answers, but the mall was closing soon, and I wanted to find my car and get my stuff before they left. I didn't want Bobby to catch me fishing through their car...well, my car.

I had the guys split up to find it faster, and it didn't take long. I was happy to find my extra key still in the magnet holder under the back of the car. I quickly found my purse thrown into the back seat, and I childishly hugged it. It was nice to have all my things back: my driver's license, debit card, cell phone, all of it.

"Okay, we can go now," I said shutting the door.

"You're not taking your car?" Brian asked.

"No. I don't want to leave them stranded here," I answered.

"But it's your car, Em," Brian argued.

"I know, but René is risking her life to do us a favor. Stranding her here at the mall is no way to repay her, now is it?"

We walked down to the bottom level to Bo's car, and I filled them in on everything René said as we drove home.

"No! Absolutely not! You're not going back into that house!" Bo yelled.

"I think it's a good plan. They won't know it's me. I'll be in a costume, and I can wear a mask. I can slip in, get Wu, and slip back out. They'll never even know I'm there."

"No! If something were to happen, anything, if you got caught, Arlo would kill you right then and there no questions asked. You can't go, I won't allow it," Bo argued.

"And just who do you think you are giving me orders? Who says I need your permission?" I fired back.

"Don't get defensive, Em. I don't want you to go because it's a bad idea and it's dangerous," Bo said.

"Yeah, Em, I don't think I want you to go either," Brian chimed in. "This guy already tried to kill you once; I don't think he'd hesitate to do it again. You're not a cat, Em, you don't have nine lives."

I couldn't fight the both of them. I still thought it was a good plan. I crossed my arms and sat there staring at the countryside zooming past.

"We don't even know if we can trust René, for all we know she could go back and tell Arlo the whole thing. They could set a trap and grab you as soon as you walk through the door."

"I trust René," I said defensively.

Okay, well she could not tell Arlo but tell Bobby then he could go tell him. We just don't know where her loyalties are, Em."

"Fine," I said. This was the most dangerous of all the female words. It meant 'You're an idiot and I'm done talking to you' and Brian and Bo both knew it.

"We're going to Bulgaria next week, let's just wait and see if we find out anything and then we will talk about our options," Bo suggested.

No one spoke the rest of the drive really. I dug through my purse looking at all my things that I thought were lost forever. My cell phone was dead, of course. I probably had about a hundred missed calls and messages from my week at the mansion. There was still money in my wallet; I guess no one had touched it until René found it. Bo noticed me going through my things and pulled his phone out and made a call.

"Menelik, it's Bohuslav. You can cancel that photo ID if you haven't gotten to it already. I no longer need it. Yes, I still need the passport for her. Thanks, Menelik."

A passport, I'd never left the country before. I'd never even been on a plane.

The week passed quickly, I kept to myself quite a bit, even sleeping at my house a few nights. I was annoyed with Bo thinking he could tell me what to do. I thought of ways that I could go to the party and get Wu myself. I now regretted not taking back my car that night at the mall. I'm sure Bo would be expecting something like that from me anyway and would stop me. I guess I would just have to wait and see what we found out in Bulgaria. If we didn't find out anything I'm not sure if Wu would still want to leave. René said Arlo took him downstairs. I remembered what I saw down there: jail cells, torture. Maybe Wu was ready to come home now no matter what.

That week I actually wished I was still a mortal so I could help Brian. Li hadn't been feeling well, so Brian was trying to run the store. He knew less about antiques than I did. I taught him how to run the register and helped out as much as I could at night. Bo considered having Brian not go to Bulgaria with us, but in order to get a flight with as few stops as possible, Brian had purchased non-refundable tickets. Long trips were always risky for vampires. You were racing against the sun. Red-eye flights were a necessity, and it was good to have a day man with you. Our flight was shortly after sunset. We would arrive in Munich only an hour before sunrise. Then it was just a short flight the next night to a city in Bulgaria that I had trouble pronouncing.

Much to Bo's dismay, I planned to stay at my own place the day before our departure. I picked up a few things and took them over to Li's...a few groceries, some cold meds, and of course some tea egg ramen from Mama Santos'. I stayed with him a little while to keep him company then went home to pack my bags. I had to Google the weather for Germany and Bulgaria because I had no idea what kind of climate they had. I felt very naïve, I'd never been anywhere before. I started thinking about Li being sick, and alone while we were gone, and my thoughts drifted to Wu and how we could get him out of that horrible house. Before I knew it, dawn was approaching. I had my bags all packed, but I hadn't had time to go hunting. I went to bed and actually set an alarm, something I hadn't done in almost a year, hoping it would wake me from my heavy vampire sleep.

The alarm worked, jarring me awake at six thirty. The sun was down behind the mountains, but it wasn't dark yet. Bo always warned me about making sure the sun was completely set before going outside because you never knew when you might come around a mountain and get fried. When night fell, I drove Bo's car back to the shop.

"Well the boss here just sucked down two golden retrievers, so I think that means we're ready to go," Brian said then held two fingers to his lips and pretended to gag.

"Have you eaten, Em?" Bo asked ignoring Brian completely.

"No," I answered.

"Did you hunt last night?"

"No," I said again sheepishly.

"Em, you can't be that irresponsible. Although we aren't savages, we can control our hunger, but if you haven't eaten in days and something happens, like someone getting a bloody nose on the plane, for instance, it will be incredibly hard to control yourself. I have no more dogs left in the back, and we don't have time to hunt."

Right on cue, Brian walked over and held out his arm in front of me.

"No," Bo said smacking his arm away.

"Dude, shut up. You just said we don't have any other choice. Our plane leaves in an hour, we gotta go!"

Brian held his arm out again, and I took it. I hadn't realized how hungry I was until the blood filled my mouth. I didn't want to stop, but all too soon Bo said the word, and I reluctantly pulled away.

"Come on," Bo said annoyed. We loaded up the car and left.

Bo stopped at a convenience store on the way to the airport. He came back with a bag that he threw at Brian once he got back in the car. It had a banana, a bag of peanuts, and a bottle of orange juice.

"Eat it," Bo said.

I smiled at the kind gesture. Maybe Bo didn't hate Brian as much as he pretended.

"I'm not really hungry," Brian said.

"I didn't ask, blood bank, now eat it."

Well so much for that notion.

The airport was busy, and it took awhile to get through security. We didn't have to wait long for our flight. It was a new experience for me. My acute senses didn't like the pressure change as the airplane ascended, but I got use to it once we leveled off. Everyone on the plane seemed to be sleeping, including Brian. Bo took this opportunity to chide me on taking blood from Brian again. I thought it just made him jealous, but he really did have Brian's well-being in mind. He gave me a speech about the replenishment of red blood cells and how taking blood from someone too frequently can be dangerous. I hadn't thought about all that, but I wasn't a blood expert like Bo seemed to be. He also took this opportunity to give me a speech about being such a picky eater. I zoned him out.

The flight was long and horribly boring. I listened to my iPod, flipped through magazines, did a couple crosswords. I was jealous of everyone who was sleeping. I wished I could sleep. I wished we could fly during the day when I slept so soundly. Once we arrived in Munich, we left Brian at the airport with our luggage. Bo said that mortals weren't welcome at the safe house, even day men. We were in an incredible hurry. Bo didn't like being out so close to dawn. We had less than an hour to get to the safe house before sunrise. We took the train into the city of Munich and ran through the streets. I'd had liked to take our time so I could admire my surroundings, but dawn was quickly approaching.

Bo was constantly checking his watch, and it made me a little nervous. I knew from what Bo told me that the sun meant instant death, but he seemed to fear it more than a rational amount, almost like it was a phobia of his. We made it to the safe house just as the sky was beginning to lighten. All safe houses were marked with the same symbol, usually on or around the door. It was a diamond of daggers surrounding a rose...the vampire glyph. Bo knocked on a large wooden door, and a small window at the top slid open.

"Bohuslav Pavlok, requesting refuge from the sun."

"We're full," the man said in English but with a thick German accent and shut the window.

I wasn't sure what we were going to do now; the sun was almost up. Bo knocked again.

"I am nearly three hundred years old, you ignorant newborn, you know I have precedence. Now open up this door or I'll rip it off its hinges and throw you to the sun."

The door opened, and the man glared at Bo as we walked in.

"Most everyone is already sleeping; I can't get you a room."

"That's fine; we'll stay in a common room," Bo said looking at this man like he might kill him.

"End of the hall," the man said then mumbled something in German. Bo said something in return, also in German, and the man backed away and disappeared.

This building was old and poorly maintained; it was dark and smelled bad. We went to the end of the hall and found a room with a couch. Bo sat at one end and had me stretch out and lay on his lap. I laid there looking at the brown and tan vertically striped wallpaper that was peeling off the walls, and wondered if all safe houses were this unkempt.

"Bo, what did you mean you have precedence?"

"The rank structure of vampires: Antecedent, of course, have top priority, but Ectype notability goes by age. The older you are, the more power and influence you have."

"Have you ever met an Ectype older than you?" I asked.

"Just a couple," he answered. "Now get some sleep, tomorrow we will go see Angelus and hopefully get some answers."

SEVENTEEN

Bo or I neither one slept very well. We were anxious to get out of there come sundown. I guess everyone else was too because as soon as darkness fell, there was a line out the door. I saw my first female vampire there; she had short spiky hair and was dressed in gothic attire. When I saw her I smiled, happy to see someone just like me, but this girl hissed at me. Seriously, she hissed. I wasn't getting the best impression of Germany in this rundown house with rude vampires. Hopefully seeing the sites on the way back to the airport would change my view, but unfortunately, as we made it outside, there was a thick fog that made it hard to see.

We had a few hours until our flight, so we would head back toward the airport on foot and hopefully find something to eat along the way. Bo said there wasn't much wildlife in Germany, especially in this part. The vampires here lived mostly off humans, and I thought maybe that's why they weren't very friendly. The constant killing had made them lose their humanity. We'd been walking for quite awhile, and Bo was starting to complain about giving up and finding a human, but the foul smell of manure let us know we were nearing a farm. It was a pig farm. Bo wasn't pleased. He said pigs didn't taste very good; they were dirty and noisy. I think the lack of sleep was making him very cranky because I'd never heard him complain this much.

He was right about them being noisy, as soon as we approached they started grunting. When we both grabbed for one, they all started squealing loudly. We each drained one quickly and got out of there in case the noise had awoken anyone in the nearby house. Bo seemed to be a little less grouchy once he ate. He was also right about them not tasting very good. Their blood was thin and kind of watery. The consistency bothered me more than the flavor, which wasn't great either. I was really hoping they would taste like bacon or pork chops; they didn't. Back at the airport, Brian told us we both looked like hell. I tried to fix myself up in the bathroom a little. My hair was a mess, and I had some mud on my clothes from the pigs. I really just needed some good sleep. The dark circles under my eyes stood out on my pale skin making me look like the typical movie vampire.

The flight to Bulgaria was short. We rented a car and headed out toward a town called Shipka. We didn't know exactly where Angelus lived, so I wasn't sure how we were going to find him. Once in the town of Shipka, we left Brian with the car, and I followed Bo who was sniffing around.

"What are we doing?" I asked.

"We're stopping for directions," he said.

I realized he was sniffing out one of our kind, and I wondered if I would ever be able to do that. Perhaps Bo's amazing sense of smell was a special gift, and I would never be as good as he was.

We approached a man who was very dirty and shaggy looking. Bo spoke to him in a different language. They spoke back and forth for a few minutes as the man pointed and gave directions. They spoke some more, and the man pointed in a different direction. Bo pulled some gloves out of his coat pocket and handed them to the man. I wasn't sure if this was payment for the information or if Bo was just being nice. We walked in the direction that the man pointed to the second time.

"Are we going to see Angelus right now?" I asked as we walked up a grassy hillside.

"No, we need to find shelter in case we are turned away."

I looked at my watch, which I'd reset to local time when we landed; it was four a.m. We didn't have long.

"That man told me there are a series of caves up here; I want to check them out before we go see Angelus."

Over a couple rolling hills we saw the cave opening. Bo went inside to check it out, and I stayed outside admiring the landscape. It was full of rolling green hills scattered with rocks and boulders; it was breathtaking. Bo approved of the cave, so we made our way back to the car. Bo followed the man's directions to Angelus's place. I wasn't sure what I was expecting, maybe something like Arlo's mansion, but this wasn't that. We followed a dirt road alongside a simple wooden fence to a large stone cottage, no guards, no gate. The cottage was two stories, all stonework on the bottom and an off white color on the top with wood accents; it was quaint. We walked up onto the cobblestone veranda and knocked on the door. Here goes nothing, I said to myself.

A pretty woman with long dark hair and beautiful green eyes answered the door. Bo spoke to her in a foreign language, and she smiled kindly at us. I caught a glimpse of fangs; she was a vampire also. After a few more sentences she switched gears.

"Oh Americans, I speak English if you prefer. I am Marna, welcome." She smiled.

"So may we have counsel with Angelus?" Bo asked.

"You've traveled very far; you look quite weary. Come, I will show you where you can stay. Get some rest, and I will summon you tomorrow."

She led us not through the house, but around the outside of it to the right. We followed a pathway past one tiny house and to another. She opened the door and directed us inside. It was a small circular stone cottage. When I say small, I mean really small. It was one room with a sectional couch, a small table with two chairs, and a small hallway, that's it. She lit a large candle on the table and the room filled with flickering dulcet light.

"Less than two hours till dawn, you will find the downstairs quite comfortable and safe." She smiled and left.

I was happy to see that the vampires here were much friendlier than the ones in Germany. Brian plopped down on the large burgundy couch.

"Man! No electricity? No TV? This place is whack," he said.

"You want entertainment? Go get the luggage," Bo said, throwing him the keys. Brian huffed and went to go get the bags from the car. I looked around the room; it was simple. The walls were bare stone, no decorations, and no windows. It was plain but homey; the place had a very warm and welcoming atmosphere. Actually, it really reminded me of those little mushroom houses that the Smurfs lived in.

I followed the small hallway; there were two doors. One door led to a small bathroom with just a toilet and sink; it was pretty much standing room only. My closet at home was bigger than this bathroom. The other door opened to some stairs. At the bottom was another door. Bo followed me down, also curious. We found a nice size bed, queen I think, made up with a pale purple quilt. There was a small bedside table but nothing else in the room. On the other side of the room was another small bathroom with just a shower and sink.

Bo and I brought our bags downstairs, and Brian settled on the couch. I wanted to get out of my dirty clothes and take a hot shower, but given that it was candlelight only around here I assumed there was no hot water. I was pleasantly surprised that there was when I went to wash my face. It made no sense to me to have running hot water but no lights, but I wasn't going to question it. It felt great to wash the two days of travel off of me. Bo was already out cold by the time I got out, and he hadn't even undressed. I removed his shoes and crawled into bed beside him.

I awoke, fairly rested, to a knock on the door. Bo was pleased to find that the downstairs door locked. I got up and opened it; it was Brian.

"Hey, some chick just came by, a different one from last night. She brought me some food and said to be ready in an hour."

I felt bad, but I woke Bo up. I knew he was very tired and could've used a couple more hours of sleep. It was only seven p.m. The sun must have just set. I went through my luggage and got dressed, unsure what to wear. What does one wear when meeting the oldest vampire in the world, something conservative I guess. I chose jeans and a thin gray sweater.

"Put your hair in a bun," Bo told me when he came out of the bathroom. Okay, must be some cultural modesty thing I guessed. We went upstairs and sat on the couch. Now all we had to do was wait.

"Have you ever met this dude before?" Brian asked Bo.

"No," Bo answered. "Let me do all the talking. If he does speak to you, make sure you answer verbally. Don't just shake your head and look him in the eyes, and do not ask him about his age or his teeth!"

"What's wrong with his teeth?" I asked curiously.

"I don't know for sure, but they say that he is so old that his fangs have worn completely down, and he has to use a finger prick in order to feed," Bo answered.

"How old is he?" I asked.

"No one really knows," he answered.

Bo got a small wooden crate out of another suitcase he'd brought. It was a gift for Angelus. Inside was a black vase with orange men and horses on it. Bo said it was customary to bring Angelus a gift in exchange for his knowledge.

There was a knock at the door; it was Marna.

"Angelus will see you now," she said.

Bo and Brian stood up, and Marna held up her hand.

"Angelus just wants to speak to the woman; you two are to stay here," she said.

I turned around and looked at Bo nervously. Oh no, what if I screw this up? Bo brought me the small wooden crate.

"Just remember what I said," he said calmly, "you'll do fine."

EIGHTEEN

"What is your name?" Marna asked as we walked from the Smurf cottage to the house.

"Em," I answered.

"In which language would you prefer to speak with him?"

"How many languages does he speak?"

"All of them," she smiled.

Holy cow, I bet that took about a thousand years to accomplish, I thought.

"Umm English please," I said feeling uncultured.

"Remove your shoes and socks please," she requested when we got in the door. I noticed she was already barefoot, even when she was outside. We walked through a candlelit living room, again no lights, no

TV, just cozy looking furniture. We passed two women who both smiled as they walked by. "Zdrasti," they said kindly. I had no idea what that meant, so I just smiled. Smiles were universal. I'm glad everyone here was so friendly; it made me a little less nervous.

"Is this your gift?" Marna asked as we stopped at a patio door that opened to the back of the house.

"Yes," I answered.

She set it down on a table, took the top off the box, and smiled.

"Wait here please."

She took the box out the door. I watched as she walked through the yard to someone sitting on a large rock, Angelus. She handed him the box, and they talked for a moment. I couldn't tell what Angelus looked like from here because he had his back to me, but he didn't look to be very big. He had long hair that looked white. A small withered old man, I guessed. She came back and set the box back down on the table.

"He will see you now." She smiled and held her arm out for me to go to him. Oh boy, I thought.

I walked barefoot through the yard, really hoping they didn't have a dog. The grass felt nice against my toes. I heard music; Angelus was playing some kind of a harp. As I got closer, my mouth dropped open. Angelus wasn't a little old man, he was a child! Okay, so he wasn't a child, but he wasn't the little gray haired geezer I had pictured. He couldn't have been more than seventeen probably! When they said the oldest vampire in the world, I was thinking a ninety-year-old grandpa, not a seventeen-year-old that had been changed a thousand years ago. I stood there in shock for a moment while he finished his song.

"That was beautiful," I said once the music faded in the wind.

"I'm no Orpheus, but thank you." He smiled. He had a very smooth, alluring voice. The kind you heard narrating nature documentaries. It reminded me of Matthew McConaughey but a higher pitch and with a European accent. I had no idea what he was talking about, and I guess it showed on my face.

"Do you not know the tale of Orpheus and Eurydice?" he asked.

I almost shook my head in response, but I remembered what Bo had said.

"I don't think so," I answered verbally.

"Come, sit," he said, gesturing to a smaller rock beside the one he was on.

"Orpheus was the son of one of the Muses and a Thracian prince. His mother gave him the gift of music. The Thracians were the most musical of the people of Greece. But Orpheus had no rival there or anywhere, except the gods alone. There was no limit to his power when he played and sang. No one and nothing could resist him. When he first met and wooed the maiden he loved, Eurydice, I don't know, but no maiden could have resisted the power of his song. They were married, but their joy was brief. Shortly after the wedding, as the bride walked in a meadow, a viper bit her, and she died. Orpheus' grief was overwhelming. He could not endure it. He was determined to go down to the world of death and try to bring Eurydice back. He said to himself: "With my song, I will charm Demeter's daughter, I will charm the lord of the dead, moving their hearts with my melody. I will bear her away from Hades."

"He dared more than any other man ever dared for his love. He took the fearsome journey to the underworld. There he struck his lyre, and at the sound all that vast multitude were charmed to stillness. No one under the spell of his voice could refuse him anything. He drew tears down Pluto's cheek and made Hell grant what love did seek. They summoned Eurydice and gave her to him, but upon one condition: that he could not look back at her as she followed him until they had reached the upper world. The two passed through the great doors of Hades to the path which would take them out of the darkness, climbing. He knew that she must be just behind him, but he longed to give one glance to make sure. But now they were almost there, the blackness was turning gray; now he had stepped out joyfully into the daylight. Then he turned to her. It was too soon; she was still in the cavern and in an instant, she was gone. She had slipped back into the darkness.

"Desperately, he tried to rush after her and follow her down, but he was not allowed. The gods would not consent to his entering the world of the dead a second time while he was still alive. He was forced to return to the earth alone, in utter desolation. There he forsook the company of men. He wandered through the wild solitudes of Thrace, comfortless except for his lyre, playing, always playing. Until at last a band of Maenads came upon him....they slew the gentle musician, tearing him limb from limb. His pieces were gathered and placed in a tomb at the foot of Mount Olympus, and there to this day the nightingales sing more sweetly than anywhere else."

"Wow, that's a horrible story," I said before I thought about my words. I hoped I didn't offend him, but he laughed. "I mean, it's sad."

"That it is, Em from America. Forgive me; I didn't properly introduce myself. I am Angelus Beledonte," he said holding out his hand. He already knew my name, so I took his hand to shake it, and he brought it to his mouth and kissed it instead. Quoting Greek poetry, kissing my hand, the guy didn't act like a teenager.

"You're a newborn," he stated plainly.

"Yes," I answered although he wasn't really asking. "How did you know?"

"Your scent still carries a mortal aroma. How long since?"

"About a month," I answered.

"And how are you finding immortality?"

"I'm not sure yet. It's not as different as I thought it would be. I thought I'd feel completely different, like I'd be a different person, ya know."

"A person oft feels that way when facing life-altering events. We don't change, Em, only the things around us."

We sat there looking at each other for a moment in awkward silence. Now closer, I could see that his hair was blond, not white but it was very light, and he had piercing blue eyes. He was wearing what looked like hospital scrubs, and he was barefoot.

"Your hair is quite long, isn't it?" he asked.

"Yes," I answered.

"Why do you have it all bound up?"

"Umm, I thought it would look more professional this way." That wasn't necessarily the truth. Bo told me to wear it up, but I wasn't sure why.

"You thought me a stuffy old crow did you?" He smiled. "May I free if from its bonds? Do you mind?"

"Umm, no."

I turned my back to him, and he pulled the pins out and unwound my hair. Then he ran his hands through it. I thought it was a little creepy, but I was afraid to say anything that might offend him. We came all this way to see if he would answer our questions, and I didn't want to be the one to ruin it.

"Mmmm, isn't that better?" He asked still running his hands through it.

"Yes, thank you," I said a little uneasy.

"Come," he said standing up and holding out his hand to me. I warily got up and took his hand.

"Tell me, Em from America, do you know your constellations?"

"I can find the big and little dipper," I answered.

We walked hand-in-hand further into the yard, and it made me a little nervous that we were so far away from the house. He stopped and sat down on the grass then laid down on his back, so I did the same.

He pulled my hair out from under me and laid it across his chest stroking it as we spoke. We laid there, and he pointed out constellation after constellation telling me the history behind each. He knew everything about mythology. We stayed there for what felt like hours. After the stars, he asked me all about myself, my parents, and my life. I was starting to wonder if he knew I was here to ask him a question at all.

After awhile a girl came and interrupted us, speaking Bulgarian. Angelus sat up and spoke kindly back to her.

"Em, this is Lyuben, I'm sorry she doesn't speak English." She smiled and did a little curtsy type thing.

"I'm sorry, Em, I have to go, but I look forward to speaking with you more tomorrow."

Well crap, I didn't even get to our current problem with Wu or get to our questions. He helped me up off the ground and kissed my hand again.

"…Until tomorrow."

Angelus left, and Lyuben held out her hand to me. I took it. These were a very touchy-feely kind of people. Holding Lyuben's hand on the way back to the house did make me feel a little less creeped out about Angelus being so physical. She was a short girl and had a young face and dark olive complexion. Her hair was black and almost as long as mine, hers stopping halfway down her back. She was also a very pretty girl, all the women I'd seen here were. We went into the house, and she took me to a small kitchen and handed me a bag.

"It's for your day man," another woman said. Yet another gorgeous woman with beautiful hair was standing there. This one was tall with jet black curls and bright red highlights.

"I'm Niobi," she said smiling, fully exposing her fangs.

"Em," I said and reached out and shook her hand.

No wonder I'd never seen a female vampire before this trip, they were all in this house. Lyuben was mortal, though. I could smell her blood, and I realized how hungry I was.

"Where do you usually hunt around here? I need to eat," I said.

"I was just about to go myself, wait here just a moment," Niobi said. She was gone just a few minutes, and Lyuben and I had nothing to do but stand there and smile at each other. She had beautiful deep dimples. When Niobi came back, she took the crook of my arm, and we walked down a hallway to the other end of the house.

"You've been granted permission to feed in the menagerie," she said excitedly. "Guests usually aren't permitted, but our guests are usually men. It's nice to have another woman around for a change."

We stopped at an information board on a wall, and Niobi studied the board then flipped two switches from green to red beside two names then pressed a button that slid the door beside us open.

"What's that for?" I asked.

"It's for the safety of our animals, so we don't feed on them too often. We don't kill; they nourish us so in turn, we take good care of them."

We walked outside into what I guess I would call a garden; there were flowers, bushes, and trees. I hadn't seen many trees since I'd been here, it was all rolling hills of grassland. There were also columns and an arch like the remains of an ancient city, which was quite possible I guess. I saw two deer trot by in the distance, and there was a woman sitting across the way stroking a tiger, yes a tiger! She was talking to it and caressing it like it was a house cat. It really surprised me when the girl leaned over and gently bit into its shoulder.

"That's Korin," Niobi said. I watched her drink from the tiger and lick the wound when she was done. The tiger laid down beside her, and she continued to stroke its fur.

"How many female vamps live here?" I asked.

"There's just Marna, Korin, and I. Rhea, Aleena, Lyuben, Boyana, and Aylin are the mortals that live here."

"Do no other men live here?" I asked.

"No, just Angelus, he doesn't like to have men in the house."

We walked over to a pool of water and sat down. As I looked around, I saw two more tigers walking about.

"Do y'all only drink tiger blood?" I asked.

"No," she laughed. "There are other animals here: deer, panthers, leopards," she said pointing up. I looked in the tree above me to see two leopards lazily stretched across the branches, and I stiffened.

"We don't eat the peafowl, we just like having them around," she said pointing at a peacock over by the bushes.

"...although the tigers sometimes eat them, and the rabbits, and deer. Even though we feed the tigers daily, they still like to hunt."

She called out two names: Benjamin and Nala, a panther and a leopard came walking toward us. No freaking way, I thought. They both came and sat down next to her. She began stroking the panther and scratching behind its ear, talking to it kindly in a different language.

"Em, do you have a preference between the two?" she asked.

"Umm no," I said, seriously nervous to be sitting next to two huge cats. "I've never tasted either," I admitted.

"I prefer panther; it has a bit darker more relaxed flavor while I find leopard more light and energizing."

I motioned for her to take her preference, and she scooted closer to the giant black cat and whispered in his ear while continuing to stroke its fur. She bit him just in front of his shoulder, and he didn't seem to mind. She drank just a moment then pulled back and licked the wound twice then whispered to him some more.

"Now just do what I did," she said, motioning toward the leopard sitting in between us.

"What do I say to it?" I asked nervously.

"It really doesn't matter what you say; it's the tone you say it in. Her name is Nala. Just speak kindly to her and pet her."

"How do I know when to stop?" I asked.

"You are new at this, aren't you? I measure by gulps, an animal this size I usually stop at four to five gulps."

I scooted a little closer to the cat and reached out my hand. She turned to sniff it and then licked me with her sandpaper tongue.

"Hey, Nala, you're a good kitty. Please don't rip my head off, okay. I'm going to bite you, but please don't bite me back," I said stroking her fur. Niobi giggled. I leaned in and tried to bite her right where Niobi had bitten Benjamin, and she didn't move a bit. I took in four mouthfuls of blood and stopped. I pulled back and licked her against the grain of her fur and got half a dozen hairs in my mouth, yuck. I went with the grain for the next one then sat up to pull the course cat hair off my tongue.

"Now thank her for the gift of her blood," Niobi said kindly.

I stroked Nala a few more times and thanked her. I really liked how they did things around here.

We went back into the house to the small kitchen from which we left. More girls were in the room sitting around a table:

Lyuben, Marna, and the two girls who had spoken to me earlier. Marna introduced them as Rhea and Aleena. They were young and pretty, late teens early twenties probably. Marna invited me to sit and play a game of cards with them. The mortals in the house didn't speak any English, but the immortals did and gladly translated for us. Before I knew it, the night was almost over, and dawn would soon be approaching. I excused myself to head back to my little Smurf house, but Aleena jumped up and started rambling something in Bulgarian. Rhea joined in, and both girls chattered about something excitedly. I didn't understand a word of it. Marna smiled and said that they would like for me to come with them to the hot springs tomorrow. I told them maybe. I was supposed to talk to Angelus again tomorrow, and hopefully, I would get to ask my questions. I found my way to the front door easily; the house was fairly large but had a simple layout.

As soon as I stepped through the door of our Smurf house, Bo was at my side in a flash, and it reminded me of our first conversation in his office when he asked me to come work for him.

"What happened? You've been gone all night!"

"Yeah," Brian chimed in from the couch, "Bo's been wiggin' out big time."

"Shut up," Bo snapped at him.

"Well, I talked to him," I said, walking over to sit next to Brian on the couch and handing him the bag of food Lyuben had given me.

"And...?" Bo asked.

"I didn't get around to asking him yet."

"Why not?" Bo asked.

"Well, we were talking about a bunch of other stuff, and I didn't want to seem rude or impatient."

"So what was he like?" Brian asked opening the bag and taking out a sandwich and some fruit.

"Well, he's not old, that shocked me. I thought he would be a withered old man kind of like that guy on the Gremlins, ya know. Or like Gandalf or something, but he's a teenager!"

"Really?" Brian said with a mouthful of food. "...but he's the oldest vampire in the world?"

"I guess." I shrugged.

"Angelus is an incredibly old Antecedent," Bo told us. "Seeds are changed when they come of age, but centuries ago a boy was considered a man much younger than by today's standards."

"He seems perfectly normal," I continued. "Everyone is very friendly, but they're a very touchy feely kind of family. I've never been touched so much by strangers," I laughed.

"Em, what happened to your hair, it was up when you left?" Bo said.

"Oh, Angelus took it down. I think he has something against hair ties, everybody wears their hair long and down in there, even Angelus' hair is down to his shoulders."

"That's because Angelus has a massive hair fetish! That's why I told you to put it up," Bo said pacing the floor.

Okay, well that makes some sense, I thought.

"Uh oh, Em, you're in trouble," Brian laughed.

"I thought I told you to shut up," Bo snapped. "We have just a little time before dawn to go hunt."

"I already ate," I said feeling a little bad that he'd been waiting for me.

"Ate what, where?" he asked.

"Um...I had some leopard a little while ago."

"That's so dope," Brian said.

Bo paced back and forth a couple more times, restlessly.

"Okay, I have to go hunt," he said, looking distraught. "I'll be back shortly."

He walked out the door, and Brian turned his head to look at me.

"See, what'd I tell ya...totally wiggin' out."

I was asleep by the time Bo returned. It's been a busy day, and I assumed tomorrow would be equally so. The next day at eight p.m. Brian called down the stairs.

"Em, there's another hot girl here for you." I was already dressed and ready to go. Bo had just gotten up.

"Please put your hair up, Em," was all he said to me. I grabbed a scrunchie and pulled it up into a messy bun and kissed him on the cheek as I passed.

Upstairs, Aleena was standing just inside the door, and Brian was unpacking a breakfast that she'd brought for him. Aleena had the lightest hair among all the girls and still it was a medium brown. She had very large green eyes and a girlish smile that I'm sure made her look younger than she was. All the girls in the house looked to be late teens and early to mid-twenties. She excitedly grabbed my hand, and we walked to the house. I made sure to take off my shoes at the door. I wouldn't have bothered putting them on at all. No one else seemed to ever wear them, but they had mentioned going to the hot springs so I thought I might need them.

She led me to a room inside the house; it was a sewing room. There were four sewing machines and bolts of fabric hanging on the wall. I suddenly realized why all their clothes were so simple and plain; they made them themselves. Angelus had been wearing cloth pants and a tunic type shirt that looked like hospital scrubs. Niobi wore black cloth pants yesterday with a silver tank top that was store bought. Right now Aleena was wearing a blue and green gypsy skirt with a blue camisole. She grabbed something off the working table in the middle of the room and turned around excitedly. She was holding an orange and white skirt layered with a pale brown.

"Oh it's beautiful," I said.

She pushed it to me, and I realized she had made it for me.

She went to close the door, and I took the hint that she wanted me to try it on. I took off my green capris and slipped the skirt on; it fit perfectly. I smiled at her and turned around to model it for her. The white t-shirt I was wearing matched, so I decided to keep the skirt on; I figured that was the perfect way to say thank you and that I liked the gift. One of the best things about being a vampire is that I rarely had to shave my legs, one less thing to worry about.

I followed Aleena back down the hallway, and I paused to look into the library. It wasn't a huge room, not like at Arlo's mansion, but it had a lot of books. What caught my attention were large display cases hanging from the ceiling that held what looked like large scrolls. It was very interesting, and I wondered what they said. There was no way they were written in English, though, so I kept walking, following the music we heard playing. We walked into a music room where Angelus was sitting at the piano playing beautifully; Marna was playing a large harp, and Rhea a violin. It all sounded wonderful together. Rhea stopped when I walked into the room and started fussing in Bulgarian. I didn't know what I did, but she was pointing at me and speaking angrily.

The others stopped playing and with a single word from Angelus, Rhea stopped talking immediately. A conversation went on that I couldn't understand, and finally, Marna spoke in English.

"Rhea is upset that Aleena has already given you their gift. They took equal part in making it for you."

"Oh, well thank you. I love it," I said not knowing if she could understand me at all.

Angelus motioned for me to come sit with him, and I did so. Angelus wasn't intimidating, but he was the type of person people listened to and obeyed. His presence dominated a room without saying a word, but I couldn't pinpoint the reason for it. There was just something regal and sophisticated about him. Like a prince.

"Do you play an instrument?" he asked me.

Uh oh, I knew how well my answer was going to go over, seeing how everyone here was sitting at an instrument and playing it perfectly.

"No, I'm sorry, I don't," I admitted.

"That is a travesty. Music is moral law. It gives soul to the universe, wings to the mind, flight to the imagination, and charm and gaiety to life and to everything."

I suddenly felt horribly inferior looking at the other faces in the room. Angelus closed his eyes and went on to play the piano feeling the music, but no one else joined in. They all watched as he played a hauntingly beautiful song that commanded an audience. His long fingers danced across the keys, and I noticed a lethal looking ring on his thumb that came to a sharp point. I hadn't noticed it the night before. It must be the 'thumb prick' Bo had mentioned. The thing he had to use for eating. When the song was over Angelus opened just one eye and looked at the other girls.

"If we're going to the hot spring we should leave soon," he said, and the girls smiled with delight. It was odd because he didn't seem like a teenager at all, he seemed to be almost a father figure in this household. I wondered about his relationship with the girls, but that was never a question I would ask. It was far too personal and none of my business.

Nobody else put on shoes, so I left mine by the door; I assumed it wasn't far. We walked up into the mountains and Angelus offered me his arm while we walked so I slipped my hand through the crook of his elbow.

"What did you think of our menagerie, my dear?"

"I loved it! I've been struggling with having to kill things, and I love being able to feed without having to."

"That is an obstacle for all new vampires; most overcome it in a decade or so," he said.

"Did you have that problem also?" I asked.

"I'm sure I did," he answered.

"Do you not remember?"

"No, that was a very long time ago," he smiled.

"So you don't remember being mortal?"

"No, not at all," he laughed. "You see, Em, the brains capacity is finite. It cannot hold unlimited memories; it has its limits. So things of little significance and ancient occurrences fade away to make room for new things. I have found that immortals start losing their mortal memories between one hundred fifty and two hundred years old. Marna is nearly two hundred and is starting to lose recollection."

So many times I found it hard to believe that Bo couldn't remember his life, but Angelus explained it in a way that made perfect sense. It made me a little sad, though; I didn't want to lose my memories. In two hundred years I wouldn't remember my parents at all. It was a struggle to remember them already since they died when I was so young.

"Because I could not stop for death, he kindly stopped for me; the carriage held but just ourselves and immortality."

Angelus often spoke in poetry, there was something endearing yet strange about it.

We walked about a mile, and I wished I'd worn my shoes. We topped the hill, and there was a steaming pond in front of us. It was big enough to fit a hundred people probably. I hadn't really thought about what we were going to do once we got here until Angelus started taking off his clothes, oh and the guy didn't wear underwear.

I turned my back quickly only to see the girls stripping their clothes off as well, and slowly slipping into the water. Aleena was waving at me to come in and join them. Awkward!

"Come in, Em," Angelus said. "I have seen many women's bodies in my lifetime. Yours is no different. Don't give it any thought."

"Angelus, don't you see she is shy," Marna chimed in. "Turn your back for her."

"Very well," he said smiling and turned his back for me. I wasn't all that shy. I just wasn't sure how I felt about being naked in a pool of water with a bunch of people I barely knew, but what the heck. I stripped off my clothes and got in the water.

I could smell the water coming up the hill, but once I got in, the sulfur assaulted my acute sense of smell but the harshness slowly faded, and my body relaxed in the hot water. We sat talking, and Marna translated. I had finally met all the girls, Boyana and Aylin were both very quiet and almost never spoke. Korin, the girl I'd watched in the menagerie, was the most abrasive of the household. She wasn't unfriendly really, just very short and not nearly as warm and inviting as the other girls. As we talked, the subject of becoming an immortal came up, and I better understood Korin's demeanor with the telling of her story. She'd been turned by an Antecedent who told her that such beauty shouldn't fade and die, so he changed her and left her, telling her nothing of what she had become or how to live. That was in 1902.

I was surprised to find out that Niobi was only ninety; she'd been born in the roaring twenties and lived with her maker until he met the sun. She gave no other details, and I assumed she cared about him a great deal and was still hurt by the incident. Marna had trouble recalling the exact details but remembered that she had been deathly sick, and the change saved her life.

They all looked at me now to tell my story, and I thought it would be the perfect way to introduce my question to Angelus. I told how Wu had been taken against his will, and I'd gone after him. Only Wu knew the real reason for me going to the mansion; René knew a half truth. I'd told this story so many times I was beginning to believe it myself. I told of how Wu saved my life and was being held captive, how Arlo nearly killed me, and Wu again saved me by giving me his blood. Everyone was quiet except for Marna who was quickly relaying my story for the other girls. I was about to ask Angelus why Arlo would want to hold Wu there and what Li had to do with any of it when Angelus went rigid.

"Hold!" he said, sitting upright in the water.

Someone was approaching; I could hear it, but I couldn't smell anything over the strong smell of the water.

TWENTY-ONE

It was Bo. He came walking up the hill and stopped at the edge of the water next to me.

"Good evening friend," Angelus said. "I do not wish to be rude, but as you can see my wives are unclothed, so I'd ask that you, please excuse yourself."

"Yes, I can see how that would pose a problem, but you see this one is not your wife! This one belongs to me," Bo said.

"Does she?" Angelus asked.

"Indeed," Bo answered.

"Is it just her body that belongs to you or her heart as well?"

Bo didn't say anything.

"Do you love her?" Angelus asked.

"I do," Bo answered.

"Then if the situation vexes you by all means take your love from here with no ill will."

Bo held his hand down to me; I didn't take it but pulled myself out of the water. I grabbed my clothes and put them on as I walked down the hill. I waited till we would be out of earshot before I spoke.

"What the hell was that, Bo? I was just about to ask him about Wu, you know, the question that we traveled all this way to ask him. You could've just ruined everything!"

"I'm not going to sit idly by while that poetic playboy puts the moves on you," he protested.

"He's not putting the moves on me!"

"Yes, he is. He's trying to recruit you for his strange little harem he's got going on here."

I admit I was a little shocked that Angelus referred to the girls as his wives. I figured they were just a coven of vampires living together as a family, not a polygamy palace.

"Why do you care, Bo? Why do you care more about me as a vampire than you did when I was mortal?"

Isn't it just like a man to finally admit that he has feelings for you after you've completely given up on him?

"It's different now," he replied.

"How so?"

"I still wanted you as a mortal, but what's the point of getting attached to someone who's just going to die. You have no idea what that's like yet, Em. Once you've lived for more than one lifetime everybody you know will die. That just happens over and over so you learn not to get attached to the mortals."

"Was it true, what you said to Angelus, do you love me?" I stopped on the hillside to look at him.

"Come on, Em, you know I do," he answered.

"Umm, how exactly am I supposed to know that? You've never said it before!"

"I've always taken care of you haven't I?"

"That's not the same thing," I protested.

"Are you hungry," he asked changing the subject.

"Yes, I could definitely kill something right now," I said, annoyed.

We walked back to the house in a tense silence. I grabbed my shoes from inside the door and then we took off over the rolling hills running quickly in search of something to eat.

It was easy running here without many obstacles. There were very few trees; you just had to dodge the rocks and the occasional boulder. We ran for a long time but I didn't mind, it felt good to run. Wild animals seemed very scarce over here, and I wondered if all the vamps fed on humans. Maybe that's why there were so many more stories and legends of vampires here than in the U.S. We finally came upon some goats after running for miles. Bo grabbed a single goat and drained it where I took just a little blood from three different ones so that I didn't kill them. Bo just laughed and shook his head. I liked this way of feeding and would love to have my own little tiger garden at home, but I knew that was impossible.

I didn't care for goat; they tasted like Grape Nuts. I really hated Grape Nuts. One memory from my childhood, I remember asking my mom to buy me some because I thought they would taste like ground up granola bars…they don't! She told me that I wouldn't like them, but I still begged and begged for her to buy them for me. So when she did, and I hated them, she still made me eat the whole box. It was horrible, but I smiled at the memory of my mother and her stubbornness. I got it honest. I lay there in the grass thinking of my mother. Bo was lying silently beside me. I didn't want to lose the memories of my parents.

"Bo, what's the oldest thing you can remember?"

He was quiet for a few moments before he answered.

"I think probably the famine of the 1860's."

I did the math in my head, which was about what Angelus said you could retain, between one hundred and fifty to two hundred years of information. So almost half of Bo's life he could no longer remember. I found that horribly depressing.

"So many left Lithuania then," he continued. "That was just before the war. Humans as food were plentiful. It was almost humane to kill back then. A quick death was far better than starving to death."

"Was that World War I, when you said you came to the U.S.?"

"You really don't know your history do you?" he laughed. "That was the Great Turkish war. I didn't leave until the Germans invaded Lithuania during the Second World War, almost one hundred years later. I'd grown tired of war."

We lay there in silence for a long while, both of us lost in our own thoughts and memories. It was only midnight when we started back to the house. I assumed my chance to talk to Angelus tonight had been completely ruined, and I was annoyed by this. We came all this way, and I'd been waiting for the right moment to bring it up all this time. When the opportunity did finally present itself, Bo ruined it.

Back at the Smurf house Bo, Brian, and I sat on the couch talking about the details of returning home, when we might leave, and what route to take home. Brian was looking at plane tickets on his phone. He'd been happy to find a wall outlet. The houses had power, just not lights. Niobi told me that Angelus much-preferred candlelight to artificial light.

There was a knock at the door, and Brian got up to answer assuming it was one of the girls bringing him some food.

"Ah…guys," Brian said from the door. It was Angelus. Bo and I both stood up from the couch and walked over.

"This is Brian," I said. "Our day man."

"Lord Brian," Angelus greeted. Then he said something in another language to Bo, and Bo answered back. After a few more words the suspense was killing me.

"Can y'all speak English please," I requested.

"Ask your question," Angelus told me.

"My friend that was taken and changed, why would Arlo want to hold him there until his grandfather died? What does his grandfather have to do with anything?"

Angelus gestured for us to sit down; Brian and I did so, but Bo remained standing.

"The information I am about to tell you is heavily guarded. There are many that hold fast to the notion that all seeds should be changed and have no choice in the matter, that they are obligated to ensure the survival of our kind. Many fear that if given the choice, Antecedents will die out completely and therefore vampires altogether. I assume the grandfather is unchanged?"

"Yes," I answered.

"What of the father?" he asked.

"His father is dead," I answered.

"Then the grandfather is the last hope."

"Last hope for what?" I wasn't following where this was going.

"It is possible to become mortal again."

We all just sat there staring at Angelus for a minute, no one speaking.

"How," Bo finally said breaking the silence.

"The same as it is done, it can be undone."

"What do you mean?" I asked.

"If the father or in this case, the grandfather is unchanged he who has been changed may drink from his mortal ancestor and become mortal again."

Again, we sat there in silence thinking about what we'd just been told.

"What about Ectypes?" I asked.

"This only pertains to Antecedents. There is no going back for an Ectype."

"So, Wu can drink his grandfather's blood and become mortal again?" I asked making sure I was hearing him right.

"Yes," he answered.

I realized why he said this was well-guarded information. This was a game changer. Any seed who didn't want to be an Antecedent could switch back, given that their fathers or grandfathers hadn't been changed already. I started wondering how rare an occasion it was for this to happen; for an Antecedent to have an unchanged father or grandfather. It probably didn't happen very often.

"We need to get back to the states. We have to tell Wu," Bo said. "Brian, get us a flight."

"Em," Angelus said. "Might you take a walk with me?"

I looked at Bo out of the corner of my eye to judge his reaction. I knew he wouldn't like it, but he didn't say anything. He and Brian would be busy making travel plans, and dawn wasn't too far away so I knew we wouldn't be flying out tonight.

"Sure," I answered, and we walked outside together.

Angelus and I walked through the house and out into the tiger garden. There we sat on the wall that looked like ancient city ruins.

"Your hair is all bound up again," he said reaching for it. He didn't ask for permission, this time, just unwound it and removed my scrunchie then ran his hands through it.

"I'm sorry about Bo earlier; he thinks you want me to stay here with you, so he's a little defensive I guess."

"Don't apologize. I have much respect for a man who fights for whom he loves." He sat there playing with my hair for a few minutes.

"He is not wrong, Em. I would very much like for you to stay here with us."

215

Okay, not sure what to say to that. I'm not going to tell Bo he was right; I'll never live it down.

"I appreciate the offer, but I want to go back home. I need to help my friend Wu."

"I understand," he said lightly. "You would be much safer here." He stared off in a daze for a moment before speaking again. "Please be careful, Em, I fear you'll be in danger back home."

"Yes, I realize saving him will be dangerous, but I must try. He's saved my life twice already, so I just can't leave him there."

"He has, and he will once more," he stared off into space again…"but the wind of death comes in a fiery wave. Love will shackle all to ashes, great love proven by great sacrifice. Beware the black bird for he surely brings death."

I may never understand Angelus' poetry. Sometimes it was really weird. I checked my watch; it wasn't long before dawn.

"I'm going to turn in," I said.

"Yes, I should as well."

We both stood up, and I took a few steps toward the house, but Angelus didn't follow.

"Are you not coming?" I asked.

"I don't sleep in the house," he said.

"Where do you sleep?"

"I take refuge in the womb of the earth," he answered.

Ok, so Angelus was a little strange, but he was a nice guy.

"Would you like to join me there?" he asked with a playful smile on his face.

"Umm, no thanks. I'll see you tomorrow." I walked quickly back to the house. Once inside, I was making my way to the door when Korin stopped to ask me in her spotty English where Angelus was; she had either a Russian or German accent which added to her edginess.

"Umm, I believe he crawled up inside Earth's womb, wherever that is."

She laughed, "A cave, he sleeps in a cave."

Okay, that made more sense now. I said my goodnights and went back to Bo and Brian. Brian was on his phone relaying flight info to Bo who was pacing the floor. The air was tense.

"Hey, Em, we'll be stopping in Paris," Brian said smiling. "I figured you'd love that."

"Sounds great," I said. Anything was better than Munich.

"When are we leaving?" I asked.

"Tomorrow," Brian answered.

"Yes, you should get some rest, Em," Bo said.

He was in a mood, I could tell. I didn't know if it was because I left with Angelus or something else, but all the tense energy in the room was radiating from Bo. I was feeling a bit overwhelmed myself with the information we'd been given, so I went downstairs to let the guys make the travel plans.

The next day Bo was still sleeping as I showered and got dressed and ready for the day. He was completely silent as we packed our things and went upstairs. We hadn't gotten our usual sunset wake-up call from one of the girls, so I figured Angelus assumed we were leaving today. It was nice to sleep in. We had a few hours before our flight, but it was over an hour drive to the airport. We made sure we left the Smurf house just the way we'd found it and walked out to put our bags in the rental car. Outside we heard voices arguing, and we watched as Angelus walked out of the other Smurf house holding a man by his throat, scolding him in another language. I couldn't imagine what someone could do to make Angelus so angry.

He was holding the man a few inches off the ground, and his thumb prick had pierced the man's skin, so a small stream of blood was running down his neck. As we stood there watching, another man came running out of the Smurf house toward Angelus.

"Look out!" I shouted.

I don't even know if he heard me because he didn't look away from the man he was holding, but he reached out his other hand behind him, and just like the man running had hit a brick wall Angelus now had him by the neck as well. Bo called to him in another language; I assumed asking him if he needed help. Angelus gave a short reply and looked at both men holding them both at arms-length. He said something else to them then clunked their heads together and let them fall to the ground. Well, this was definitely a side of him I hadn't seen. Angelus stepped inside the Smurf house and walked out carrying Rhea. I better understood the situation and hoped that she wasn't hurt. Angelus said something to Bo as he carried Rhea inside.

"Come on," Bo said, setting down our bags and walking toward the men laying on the ground.

"What are we doing?" I asked.

"Angelus has asked us to take out the trash," he replied. "We can put our bags in the backseat and the men in the trunk."

Bo grabbed one man, and Brian and I grabbed the other putting them into the trunk. A few moments later Angelus came back out with all the girls except Rhea, to say goodbye. I asked if she was okay.

"She's fine," Angelus told me. "She just had a scare; that is all. Those men thought they could put their hands on her. They have been educated otherwise. I'm sorry you had to see that, Em."

"That's fine," I said. "You do what you gotta do."

I hugged all the girls; Marna had us exchange addresses so that we could keep in touch.

Angelus hugged me then while holding both sides of my face gave me more of his poetic babble:

"When old age shall this generation waste, thou shalt remain in the midst of other woe. Than ours a friend to man, to whom thou say'st, beauty is truth, truth beauty, that is all ye need to know on earth, and all ye need to know."

Then he kissed me right on the lips. I thought if Bo had seen him there might have been one more body to put into the trunk, but he wasn't paying attention. I wondered how the women kept from getting jealous of each other and if not over each other, over me. Watching their husband kiss a stranger must be a little uncomfortable. They didn't seem to mind, and I think they would have all been happy for me to take Angelus up on his offer and live there with them.

We said our goodbyes and left. About halfway to the airport, the guys in the trunk started hollering and beating on the car. I looked at Bo.

"We'll let them out in just a little while." Another twenty minutes down the road Bo pulled over and popped the trunk. The men got out fussing in their foreign language slamming the trunk shut then flipped us off as we pulled back onto the road.

We had time to kill at the airport, and Brian said he was excited to get some real food. Brian was a burger and fries kind of guy, and Angelus' girls were fruit and vegetable people.

Bo was still extremely quiet and that continued throughout our three-hour flight and on into the city of Paris. We had a couple hours to look around before going to the safe house. I was in a wonderful mood as we walked through the city seeing the sites even though Bo was being a stick in the mud. He definitely put a damper on my mood when he pointed out the obvious.

"We're in the city, Em, we're not going to find any animals, we'll have to take a human tonight."

I knew he was right; I didn't like the idea, but I knew we didn't have any other options.

"We'll find a homeless person, they probably won't live through the winter anyway," he said trying to make me feel better.

It was around four a.m., and the metro was a ghost town. We had our pick, as there were at least a dozen people scattered about sleeping on the ground. Bo was sniffing the air trying to find the most appealing of them, and I tried to do the same. I let him take the first bite, and I turned my head so I didn't have to see the struggle between them. Then Bo called me to finish him, and I reluctantly did so. This ruined my night. I didn't like killing anything, let alone people. Leaving the body there on the ground where we found him, we walked in silence to the safe house.

This house was in much better shape than the one in Munich. There was no trouble getting in the door. The others here kept to themselves, and no one spoke to us as we went to our room. The décor was tacky and reminded me of an old French whore house, and perhaps it used to be or even still was. We rested more easily here being in an actual room with a lock on the door. I don't think Bo slept much at all in the safe house in Munich. I think he fought it as hard as he could to stay as vigilant as possible to protect us while I slept.

We both laid down on the bed, and I couldn't stand his silence anymore, I had to know what was on his mind, so I asked him flat out what was bothering him.

"I'm just thinking, Em. I'm just thinking," he said and wrapped his arms around me holding me tightly. I knew there was definitely something wrong, but I would let it go until he wanted to talk about it.

It was great to be home after another long flight. We had the time zones on our side for the return trip, so we weren't quite as pressed for time, but we didn't have long before dawn. We needed to hunt, and Bo insisted that we stay close to home and once again take a human for our meal. As we walked, I complained about having to kill another person.

"You're going to have to kill more humans, Em, a lot of them, for the next couple weeks," he said earnestly.

"Why?" I asked in horror.

"We need to mask your scent as much as possible."

"What are you talking about?"

"If I'm going to send you back into that house, I'm going to take every precaution there is."

"That's what you've been worrying about?"

Bo grabbed me and hugged me, a tight smothering hug.

"I don't like it, Em, I don't like it at all, but I can't think of any other way than the party."

"Okay," I said, my face smushed into his shoulder, and he loosened his grip on me a little.

"I don't like putting you in danger," he said.

"Yeah, unless it's baiting me for my first kill," I said sarcastically. "Oh hey, can we do it that way," I asked. "...bait in the sleaze balls?"

"Yes, we can do that, but not tonight. We don't have time; we have to be quick. I think we should dive into some combat training as well."

I was feeling pretty good the next day despite having to kill a human the night before. I was happy to be home. Bo checked upstairs and found that the store had remained closed the whole time we were gone, so we went to go check on Li before it got too late. We drove to his place, and I was thankful Bo had a remote to control the UV floodlights, they were nauseating! We knocked, but he didn't answer. Bo used his key, and we went inside wondering if he was too sick to get out of bed, but he wasn't there. He hadn't been at the shop for the last week, and he wasn't at home either. Li didn't go much of anywhere else, and his car was in the driveway. It was almost midnight and unlike him to be out at this hour. Something was wrong.

Bo and I drove around and checked the couple other places that he could possibly be and found nothing. We were hoping he hadn't been picked up or killed by Arlo's men. He had a pretty bad cold when we left, and now I felt bad for leaving him alone. Reluctantly, we drove to the hospital to check there. The receptionist told us he'd been admitted two days ago, and the doctor wanted to talk to his family when they arrived. A young, pretty doctor came and introduced herself as Dr. Snyder. She was hoping for an actual family member, but we told her that Li's grandson was still out of town and beyond reach, but we were trying to get in touch with him. She told us that Li had developed pneumonia which was quite dangerous for a man his age. They were giving him oxygen treatments and had him on antibiotics, but the situation was serious, and he was at risk of respiratory failure. Bo and I just looked at each other. We had to rescue Wu, ASAP!

Back at the shop Bo, Brian, and I sat there in the office none of us saying anything. The situation was critical. Li was the only way Wu could become mortal again, and he was very sick and could possibly die. Aside from the possibility of changing Wu back, Li could die without Wu being here, without saying goodbye. There was nothing we could do; the party wasn't for another two weeks. Going there before the party was out of the question. That was far too dangerous. There was no other way to get in touch with Wu or René. We tried throwing around ideas, but there really were no other options. Begging Arlo to release Wu, telling him his grandfather was on his deathbed. Morse code into Wu's window, to which Bo told Brian was the stupidest idea he'd ever heard. Me trying to catch René outside and talk through the fence. All these ideas were bad ones. We would have to wait till the Halloween party and just hope that Li could hold on that long.

We dove into combat and defense training like Bo suggested. I fought Bo and Brian both. I found that since I'd been taking in more blood every night that I was able to beat Brian more easily. I was still no match for Bo's strength and experience, though. Bo didn't hold back as Brian did.

During one night of training, Bo had given me a bloody nose, and things got physical between him and Brian. Brian didn't like it and hit Bo while screaming at him to not be so hard on me.

"I'm trying to help her! She'll never learn if we always take it easy on her!" he yelled back.

"I'm not going to stand here and watch this," Brian said.

"You think I enjoy this? You think you love her more than I do? If you don't want to watch then leave, otherwise sit down and stay out of the way!"

Moods around here were tense, we all felt it. We were all worried that we wouldn't be able to get to Wu before Li died. In the meantime, Bo and I had become a perfect scum bag killing machine. We had our routine down. I would walk down a darkened street or alleyway, and like flies to honey, the perverts and deviants would come around in hopes to rob, rape, or murder me. If it was just one man, Bo would sit back and let me handle it trying to hone my fighting skills. If there was more than one, he would stay very close, just beyond the shadows to jump in if I needed him. I was gaining great confidence in my fighting abilities.

I found it much easier to kill when I was being attacked. Instinct kicked in I guess, kill or be killed. I didn't feel bad about killing people like this, because if it wasn't me they attacked it would be the next girl who may not be able to handle herself as well. I learned a lot from hunting like this. I learned a lot about myself, my strengths, and my weaknesses. I developed a keener sense of smell because of it. Bo was right; you couldn't really smell blood until you tasted it. He even had me drink from a drunk man one night just to know what it feels like when you do and see how my body would react to alcohol-infused blood. I blacked out, and Bo had to carry me home, but now I knew what it smelt like and tasted like, and I could avoid it. Bo taught me so much.

We fell into a routine: visit Li, training, plan for the night of the party, and go hunting...every night. Bo hated that he couldn't go into the mansion with me. They would know him, smell him. He said he wanted me to feed as much as possible until then. He said human blood covers your scent better than animal blood. 'You are what you eat' he told me. They only knew me as a mortal there so hopefully now that I was a vampire I wouldn't smell the same. Brian, they didn't know at all. It was a little risky taking him inside, but they would assume he was my day man or lover, and he should be safe from harm. He definitely wouldn't be the only mortal in the house, and Bo didn't want me going in alone.

We went over and over plans to get in and out, accounting for different problems along the way, just like we had done with the meeting with René. Hopefully, this operation would be as fast and simple as that one had been. We would go in, find Wu as quickly as possible, and get out. I would have to find some kind of costume that would hide my face, but I could move in easily. Then I remembered Wu's costume that he'd worn to the costume party at Outer Moon. He'd been a ninja, with nothing showing but his eyes. That'd be perfect and may actually work to my advantage in that he might recognize his own costume. Bo said a samurai sword would go with my costume, and I could carry it for extra protection. He had me train with one, but I was absolutely horrible at it. I wouldn't carry it with me because I thought given my lack of skill with it, it would slow me down more than help me.

Bo told Brian that he was working on an idea for his costume and when he revealed it we both loved it. It was a Ghost Buster uniform complete with a proton pack. We knew Bo had been up to something else, though...the proton pack was really a flame thrower. It was a little heavy but worked really well with the costume, so you'd never know its secret. Bo was really pulling out all the stops. I thought something like that would be impossible to get, but Bo said it was rather easy for an antique dealer as they were widely used during World War II. Bo had Brian take it out in the parking lot and try it out while we stayed inside. Really, there was no greater weapon against a vampire. I felt like the odds were in our favor.

The two weeks passed quickly: training and hunting. Li was getting worse. The doctor told us Li had developed acute respiratory distress syndrome. He was now on a ventilator. She gave him two to four weeks to live. We had to bring Wu back no matter what! The night of the party was fast approaching and much to our surprise, Bo suggested we drive to Charlotte the night before so we could look around and watch the place for a little while before we went in. We stayed in an old abandoned house just inside the city. Brian stayed upstairs, and we stayed in the basement. I figured none of us would get much sleep with what was coming, but we tried to rest as much as possible. At sunset, I would get up, put my costume on, and walk into Arlo's mansion once again.

Susan Stumpf

TWENTY-FOUR

I was standing beside Bo's car in the street just down the road from the mansion. In pretty much the same spot I'd watched the seed hunters at the gate just about seven weeks ago. Has it only been seven weeks? It felt like an eternity. Cars were parked all down the driveway and were now lining the street. There were a couple people walking toward the mansion in their costumes. The gate was open, and I could see people also standing in front of the house. I took a deep breath and could smell Bo in the air. He'd left a moment ago to walk the perimeter just to look around and was returning now. We'd been standing outside for awhile, and it was time for Brian and me to go in.

"Be careful," Bo said with a tortured look on his face. "I'll be around, holler if you need me and I'll come running."

"I know." I smiled. "This'll be a piece of cake."

"I hope so. Hurry back to me, Em." He wrapped his arms around me and kissed me. It was a long passionate kiss that only ended when Brian awkwardly cleared his throat then laughed. I expected Bo to say something snarky to him, but he put his hand on Brian's shoulder.

"Take care of her Brian, and you be careful as well."

"Fifty-pound pack of highly flammable material on my back, walking into a house full of vampires on Halloween night. I think careful is pretty much out the window, dude."

Bo hugged me one more time. I pulled up the mask on my costume then Brian and I walked to the house. There was another couple just walking in as we approached, and I was glad. The anticipation of waiting for the door to open after knocking would have been maddening. We followed them inside, and I was glad to see there were half a dozen people scattered in the entryway talking and laughing. We could blend in with more people around.

"Okay, so let's stand here for a few minutes and see where the most traffic is flowing," I said. I assume the ballroom was where most of the action was happening. I remembered it was in the west wing, but I couldn't remember which hallway.

People were coming and going from both hallways. Wu obviously wasn't out here, so we took one hallway and went with the flow of people. Some were going to the sitting room; there were drinks and appetizers for the mortals. We stepped into the room for just a moment to scan the occupants and see if we could spot Wu. Only a few people had costumes that completely covered their faces, but I was pretty sure he wasn't in here. We followed the flow of people farther down this hallway to the ballroom. There were a lot more people in here, so it took much longer to scan the crowd. I didn't see Wu, but I did spot Arlo dressed in all black and wearing a feathered cape and a beak hat. What was he a crow? More like a vulture, if you ask me. Then I remembered something Angelus said in the midst of his poetic garble 'Beware the black bird for he surely brings death.' A chill ran down my spine. I pulled Brian back toward the door.

"I guess you didn't see him in there either?" I kept pulling him farther down the hallway. I wanted as far away from Arlo as possible. I was freaking out a little bit. What else had Angelus said that night? I thought it was completely weird and meaningless at the time… something about death coming in a fiery wave, ashes and love being shown through sacrifice, I think. Angelus said I'd be safer staying with him, and that I would be in great danger back home. Did Angelus predict my own death? Was he psychic or something?

"What's wrong, babe?" Brian asked.

"I'm afraid I'm going to die here tonight. I think Angelus predicted it."

"Hey," he said lifting my chin and speaking seriously, "I won't let that happen, Em, I won't. Besides you get into trouble and…who ya gonna call?" he said patting the proton pack nozzle in the holster at his side. I had to laugh at the Ghost Busters reference. Brian always knew how to make me feel better.

"Hey, let's check that other side, and then we'll just stand in that entryway for awhile okay? That way we'll be close to the door. Will that make you feel better?" he asked.

"Yes, let's do that."

Down the other side was the piano lounge which had drawn quite a crowd as well because René was singing. We walked in and stood against the wall. René was dressed as a mermaid, and with her red hair, she looked like Ariel from the cartoon. I knew she wouldn't recognize me with my face covered, so I waited for her to make eye contact and I winked at her. When she was done with her song, she announced she was going to take a short break and would be back in a little while. She looked at me as she walked out the door, and we followed behind her.

"Em?" René whispered at me once we were in the hallway.

"Yes," I whispered back through my ninja mask. "Where's Wu? I can't find him."

"He may still be in his room. I can go check for you."

"Yes, please. I want to get out of here as quickly as possible."

René went upstairs to look for Wu, so Brian and I waited in the foyer.

"Fe. Fi. Fo. Fum," we heard coming from behind us. Oh no! I knew that voice, it was Arlo. He knew it was me. We turned around quickly. Arlo was standing there with two other men. One was Franco, the guy who had dragged me up the stairs and into Wu's room, the other had his face covered in a skull mask.

"Did you think I couldn't smell you, Emina? I've tasted your blood. I know your scent although it is different now. You found someone to turn you, to escape your pitiful mortal life I see."

We took a few steps backward as he was talking.

"I will take great pleasure in killing you…again."

"You're not going to touch her!" Brian said.

"And who is going to stop me, you?"

Brian grabbed the nozzle of his proton pack and gave the trigger a quick squeeze letting out one single fireball as a warning.

Arlo jumped back, and half a dozen vampires ran screaming from the foyer.

"Go, Em, get out of here," Brian said letting out another short fire burst. I backed away toward the door pulling on the back of his costume to come too, but somebody grabbed me from behind. It was the creepy movie villain guy who worked the security station, Dante. He didn't know what he was in for, all of Bo's combat training had paid off. I was able to get him off of me and kick him away. Brian took that opportunity to torch him. At that point, all hell broke loose.

"Go Em, go!" Brian repeated as the guy got up and started running and screaming while on fire. Brian let out another long fire burst, sweeping it across the room.

"Come on, Brian!" I shouted. I wasn't going to leave without him.

"I'll hold them off Em, you go. Go now!"

Two more men grabbed me, and I fought with them, it was Franco and the skeleton guy. Brian couldn't torch them so close to me. People were running and screaming everywhere. They had started running out the front door. The large rug in the middle of the foyer was on fire, and now the big red rug on the stairway was as well. At least two people were running around also on fire. It was complete chaos!

Brian stopped torching to come try to pull one of the two guys off of me. Arlo took this opportunity to walk up behind Brian and snap his neck right there in front of me.

"NO! I screamed.

Bo must have seen people running out because he ran in and tackled Arlo just as Brian's lifeless body fell to the floor. I pushed Franco off me and into the flames of the rug. The other guy knocked me down, and I grabbed the nozzle from Brian's dead hands and lit the guy on fire. I couldn't see Bo anywhere, but I spotted Wu at the top of the stairs. He couldn't go down them; they were completely engulfed in flames.

"Wu!" I shouted pulling down my mask. He looked at me and hopped over the banister landing hard on the floor. I ran over to him.

"Are you okay?" I asked.

"Yes, let's get out of here."

"No, Bo is in here somewhere, we have to find him."

There were still people running everywhere screaming and shouting all trying to get out the front door. We spotted Bo down the back hallway that was mostly on fire, the top filled with thick black smoke.

"Bo!" I screamed. He was still fighting with Arlo whose feather cape was now on fire.

"Get her out of here, Wu!" he shouted back to us.

They both disappeared through a door down the flaming hallway. I started to run down there to help him having to dodge a flaming picture that was falling off the wall, but Wu grabbed me by the waist.

"No, no!" I shouted. "We have to save Bo! We have to save him!"

"It's too far gone, Em, if you go down there you'll die," Wu reasoned.

"I have to try, we can't leave him, we can't!"

Wu tried pulling me back toward the foyer, but I fought him as hard as I could.

"No! We can't leave him!" I kicked and flailed with Wu's arms around my waist.

"I'm sorry, Em," Wu said, and he released me only to slip his arm around my neck. He squeezed his arms together, and that was the last thing I remembered from that night.

TWENTY-FIVE

I awoke hungry and dazed. I was weak and dizzy and felt like I was dreaming or drunk. I was starving! Nothing really existed outside of my hunger and thirst. I stumbled when I tried to stand up, so I crawled. I paid no attention to my surroundings. I only had one thing on my mind. I could hear a heart beating; I could actually hear it. It pounded in my head like a drum, a maddening drum. Food...blood... there! I bit and warm blood filled my mouth, I drank and drank and don't remember ever stopping.

"Em, Em honey, wake up. Please wake up." I knew that voice, it was Wu's soft gentle low voice.

"Wake up, Em, please."

I was awake, but my eyes didn't want to open; there was something in my mouth, something furry. My teeth were locked down on something. I opened my eyes and my mouth and tried to sit up, I was still very dizzy, my mind was clouded and heavy. I was on the floor of Bo's apartment. I looked down in horror to see Loki's lifeless body in front of me. Oh no, I ate Loki.

"Are you okay, Em?" Wu asked.

"What's wrong with me?"

"Right now you're suffering from a hemo-narcosis; it's from the lack of blood. You've been out for awhile. You're starving."

"I killed Loki," I said in horror looking down at the dog I'd taken care of all this time, Bo's guard dog.

"Em," Wu said shaking his head, "Bo ate Thor and Loki all the time, we always brought in replacements. It was just easier to name them all the same instead of constantly thinking up new names. This is probably the fourth Loki since you've been with us. Why do you think Bo fed them raw steak? They were guard dogs, yes, but they were also a special treat for Bo. I'm surprised you never noticed the difference."

"Did Bo make it out?"

"I don't think so, Em. I looked around outside for a long time hoping he would turn up, but I never found him."

"You should have let me go to him," I yelled. "You should have let me help him! We could have all gotten out together."

"Em," he said putting his hands on my face, "you know that's not true. If you had gone down that hallway, you would've never made it out. You know that. You couldn't save him, Em. I know you wanted to, but you couldn't. He sacrificed himself so that we could get out."

I knew he was right. Angelus' words came back to me again 'great love proven by great sacrifice' and I got another chill.

"I just want to sleep," I said.

"Okay, get some rest. I'll go get you some food," he said, and he carried me back to the bed.

"Oh Em, where's Umpa? He's not at home."

I pushed back the drowsiness and the languor. The importance of our mission that I'd temporarily forgotten was coming back to me. I weakly sat up in bed.

"He's in the hospital, Wu, that's why we came to rescue you. He's dying. The doctor gave him about four weeks to live, and that was two weeks ago."

Wu started to get up off the bed.

"No, wait! There's more."

I told him about how we went to see Angelus and found out that he could change back by drinking his grandfather's unchanged blood, and that was why Arlo wasn't letting him leave. Arlo didn't want a secret like that getting out. Wu just sat there staring for a minute processing the information. Then he got up, kissed me on the cheek, and left.

I didn't know how long he was gone, but I awoke to his scent and another heartbeat pounding in my head and the smell of blood. Being hungry seemed to intensify my already heightened senses. I could tell the blood was human, but the hunger trumped any concern for who they were or their life. Wu laid the person next to me on the bed, and I drank, I drank every drop. I could feel the blood pulse through my weak system strengthening me.

I felt the warmth spread over me, and I felt almost normal again.

"Better?" Wu asked.

"Yes," I answered.

"Good, because there's someone here who wants to see you," he said as he removed the body from the bed and left.

Hope blossomed in me that Bo had made it out, that he was back. A moment later René walked in, and I chided myself for being so stupid. Why would Wu ask if I was feeling better before Bo would come in? He was making sure René, a mortal, would be safe in my presence, that I was no longer hungry.

"Hey, sugah, how you feeling?" she asked.

"I'm not sure," I answered. I felt very confused. Two of the most important people in my life just died, and I felt fine. I missed them, and I wished it hadn't happened, but I wasn't devastated as I should be, and this bothered me a little bit. René was telling me how she almost hadn't made it out of the house and how Wu found her, but I was lost in my own thoughts.

I was feeling much better, so I took René to my house. There was so much irony in going through my closet to find clothes for her to wear. I knew exactly how she felt. I told her she could stay here at my house. I had an extra room, my old room. I didn't think I would be staying at my house much anyway. I longed for the safety and security of Bo's apartment.

I spent the next few days waiting and hoping that Bo would come back, that maybe he had made it out and would come back to me. I knew there was no hope for Brian. I'd watched him die right before my eyes, but not knowing what happened to Bo bothered me. I now hunted indiscriminately not caring about my prey. Bo was right, losing those you loved calloused your heart.

Wu got the call to come say his final goodbyes to his grandfather. I also said my goodbyes to Li's unresponsive body. Wu asked that I step outside the door and keep watch for him. I thought he was going to drink from Li and become mortal again, but a few moments later he slipped half a dozen large syringes full of blood into my bag and just before Dr. Snyder walked over he looked at me and said, "I kind of like being a vampire," then gave me his signature wink. I guess the blood was just in case he changed his mind one day. I wondered if it would still work if the blood wasn't fresh, we may never know.

Li wished to have his body buried in Okinawa, the land of his grandfathers, and Wu invited me to travel with him. At first, I declined, but then I decided to travel part of the way with him, then go on to Bulgaria to get some answers from Angelus. I wanted to know why he didn't tell me exactly what was waiting for me back home, why he only spoke in poetic riddles. If he'd told me Bo and Brian were going to die, I would have, or could have done something differently.

Wu and I parted ways in Tokyo. I was glad I was traveling with him thus far. As a newborn Ectype, I had no seniority in the safe houses and Wu had top priority being an Antecedent, even a newborn one. The safe house in Tokyo was packed, and they actually kicked someone out to make room for Wu. The next night, he went on to Okinawa, and I boarded my flight to Bulgaria. I didn't rent a car like we did last time, I felt bad using Bo's money. The nearest safe houses were in Turkey and Romania, both hours away, so I spent the remaining hours before dawn searching for a place to stay. Sitting in a cold, damp cave in a foreign country, I never felt more alone.

The next night, I ran and hitchhiked my way to Shipka; it didn't take long. Marna answered the door, as usual. She spoke the most languages, aside from Angelus, of course. She hugged me and announced my arrival to the house. The other girls came to greet me. They'd all been sitting in the living room around Angelus.

"I need to talk to you," I said to him as I absentmindedly hugged the girls. Marna, recognizing the seriousness on my face, shooed everyone out of the room so we could talk. Angelus got up from the couch and crossed the room.

"I'm glad you are well," he said putting both hands on my face.

"No thanks to you," I said backing away so his hands would fall. "Why the hell didn't you tell me what was going to happen? Why didn't you tell me, just flat out tell me?"

"I didn't know what was going to happen with any certainty," he replied.

"That's crap, Angelus! You knew about the fire! You said death was going to come in a fiery wave and that great love would be proven by great sacrifice, that the black bird would bring death. You knew what was going to happen!"

"My visions are never certain. I rarely share them with anyone for that very reason. The future is not set. Sometimes the slightest things change the directions of our lives: the merest breath of circumstance, a random moment that connects like a meteorite striking the earth. Lives have swiveled and changed direction on the strength of a chance remark."

I wanted to hit him, and he may have sensed that because he grabbed my wrists and held my hands together in front of us wrapping his long fingers over top of mine.

"Who have you lost my dear?"

"I lost them both," I replied, "I lost everything."

"Fate is never fair. You were caught in a current much stronger than yourself; struggle against it and you'll drown not just yourself but those who try to save you. Swim with it, and you will survive."

"Oh shut up, Angelus!" I wasn't in the mood for his poetic ramblings. I was cold, wet, and tired. He called for Marna to show me to a room, but before we walked out of the house, he kissed me on the forehead and whispered, "All is not lost, Em, you have a future still."

TWENTY-SIX

I felt much better after a hot shower and some sleep. I was now able to greet the girls with genuine affection. Angelus was busy with other "seekers" as they called them, so I sat and talked with the girls. They wanted to hear the story of what had happened, but I just couldn't bring myself to tell it. The girls were like a warm blanket to my soul, such love and acceptance, so much kindness. Perhaps I would stay here now that I'd lost everything. Stay and be part of the Crystal Gayle sisterhood. Could I really leave Wu alone? He'd saved my life so many times that I felt obligated to stay by his side now. I enjoyed being with the girls, but they were a little too up close and personal for my current mood. I excused myself to go for a run and hunt. I knew I was welcome to feed in the menagerie, but I just wanted to be alone. I ran for a long time and found a sheep to eat. I didn't take blood from several. I just drained a single one. I sat there running my fingers through its thick wool remembering how I'd been so opposed to such an act not so long ago.

I made my way back to the house, and Angelus was waiting for me on the couch of my cottage. I sat down next to him.

"What dies not but endures with pain…" he started.

I held up my hand to stop him. I used to find his poetic way of speaking strange yet fascinating, but anymore it was just annoying.

"Don't let this change you, Em," he began again. "Don't let it harden you. You have a warrior's heart, a warrior's heart will not endure this existence. The heart of a poet or the heart of a lover is needed to survive the heartaches of multiple lifetimes."

"How can I have the heart of a lover when those I love are taken from me?" I asked.

"You will find love again." He smiled.

255

"Have you seen it?" I asked semi-jokingly.

"I have," he replied.

"What have you seen?" I asked, wondering if he was going to lay some cheesy line on me about the two of us ending up together.

"I have seen new birth. I see children…twins, I think. I see your heart full with more love than you knew it could possess."

I looked at him confused; we both knew I was unable to have children now that I was a vampire.

"They are oriental children, but you protect them with the love and ferocity of a mother."

Wu, Wu is going to have children…seeds! They will need protecting!

"I see things more clearly and frequently when you are here, Em. You seem to magnify my visions. Stay with me, stay here with us."

"How can I stay when I know my future is to go home and protect Wu's children?"

"That is not your future, Em, it's but a possibility of your future. Only half of my visions come to pass. The future isn't written yet, the slightest of things can change the path and render the vision void."

"How maddening. So how do you ever decide anything knowing that your decision can change the path you're on and forever change your life?"

"The best thing about the future is that it comes one day at a time," he smiled.

Suddenly I felt just like Neo in the kitchen of the Oracle.

"What were your plans before I told you this?" he asked.

"I was going to stay for awhile I guess."

"Then staying wouldn't alter this path. Stay until something calls you to leave."

I would stay. I had a feeling this place would forever be a sanctuary of healing for me. I liked having a place to run away to. I found the disconnection from the rest of the world refreshing, no phones, no computer, no TV. We spent our time talking, sewing, and playing games and music. I was learning to play the piano. I was content here.

I was starting to wonder if I would ever be 'called to leave' as Angelus said. Until one day a couple weeks later there was a knock at my door. When I opened it, I couldn't believe my eyes. If I were able to dream, I would have thought that I was, but I was yet to have a dream as a vampire. Perhaps vampires didn't dream at all. I opened the door, and I couldn't speak.

"I see how it is, I'm gone for a few weeks and you run off to the pretty boy's house," Bo said.

"You're alive," was all I could say.

"Yes," he smiled.

"You're alive," I repeated, unable to put any other thoughts together other than the obvious.

"Yes," he said again.

"But how?"

"Are you disappointed?" he asked facetiously. "I could go jump into a volcano or something I guess." He turned around and took a step away from the house, but I grabbed him and hugged him for a very long time. Bo being Bo, tried to pull away a couple times, but I didn't let him. After a few minutes had passed, I asked again, "How?"

"Arlo jumped out a window, and I went after him. Lesson number five: never let your enemies live.

"But where have you been, why didn't you come home?"

"I was running down Arlo. I knew if he got away, if he lived, that he would come after you. He would want revenge. I had to find him. I had to kill him. He got away from me that night, but I tracked him down. He stayed just a few steps ahead of me for a few days, but I finally caught up with him. I would've let you guys know what was going on, but nobody seems to want to answer their phone."

I'd let my cell phone die weeks ago and hadn't bothered to charge it. Everyone who ever contacted me was dead, or so I thought. I probably should've charged it so Wu or René could get a hold of me if they had to.

"When I got home," Bo continued, "nobody was there. I waited, and Wu finally came back and told me where you went, so here I am. Once again, I have to come steal you back from this poetic playboy. I was really disappointed to hear this is where you went, Em."

"It's not like that; Angelus predicted what would happen. He predicted the fire and death. I wanted to firstly, yell at him for not telling me exactly what was going to happen. Secondly, I wanted to see if he'd seen anything else."

"…and had he?" Bo asked.

"Yes. Wu is going to be a father."

Bo made a face like he was pondering something, and I asked what it was about.

"Wu didn't come home from Japan alone. He brought two girls with him, Persia and Song, sisters. He saved them one night from a human trafficker trying to force them onto a boat. The older sister, Persia seems to be quite smitten with him."

"I bet she's the mother." I smiled. I was happy that Wu was going to have children, he deserved such happiness.

"Well, what now?" Bo asked.

"We go home," I said. "Wu's twins will need protecting, and I'm destined to do just that."

CHAPTER ONE

I stood motionless as I watched Bo crawl through the mud of a small village. He was covered in blood and filth. I wanted to go to him, but I couldn't. It was like I was a ghost. I didn't have a body. I was just a spectator. He was badly hurt and weak, I could tell. I futilely watched while he crawled into a run down looking shack, and my being followed him inside hovering overhead. I watched in horror as Bo reached for a child and bit her, draining her of her blood. I opened my mouth to scream in horror, but no sound came out. We ate humans, but not children, never children.

Susan Stumpf

This child couldn't have been more than four years old. I was outraged. The struggle between the two awoke an older sibling, a girl who looked to be around seven or eight. Bo grabbed her and drained her as well. I screamed again trying to will my ghostly being to stop him, to pull him away, to stop this horror that was happening before my eyes. Again no sound escaped my lips, and I couldn't will my ghostly form to move.

Back in reality, my screams were not silent, and Bo was frantically trying to awaken me from my sleep. I awoke disoriented and still screaming. It took me a moment to realize what was happening. I'd been a vampire for five years now, and I hadn't had a dream or nightmare since. Vampires didn't dream, or so I thought. I pulled away from Bo's arms looking at him as if he were a monster. I wasn't able to shake the terrible feeling of my dream. Bo had just as much a look of terror on his face as I imagine I did on mine.

"What's wrong?" he asked for the fifth time.

"I think I had a nightmare," I replied, backing away from his arms once again.

"That's impossible," he replied. "We don't dream."

"It was a nightmare," I said again getting out of our bed.

"What did you see?" he asked, following me to the bathroom.

"I don't want to talk about it, leave me alone," I said closing the door between us.

I had hoped a hot shower would make me feel better, but it didn't. The dream was so vivid it seemed completely real. I remembered dreams. I hadn't been a vampire so long that I'd forgotten them, forgotten what they were like. This seemed different than what I remembered. It seemed so real. I couldn't look Bo in the eye, the vision of him feeding on the children stuck with me. So, I headed to Wu's place. After Wu's grandfather Li, died, Wu sold their house that they lived in together and bought the building across the street from Forever Young Antiques where he lived with his wife, Persia and her sister Song. Angelus' vision was correct, Wu and Persia had twins: a boy and a girl, Cameron and Kimber-li. They were almost five years old now and also as predicted, I loved them dearly. There was an underground passage adjoining our building to Wu's. It was a way for us to stay connected and protect each other.

I entered the key code to the vault door that opened into the existing sewer system. The dank smell of underground assaulted my senses. I liked that the buildings were connected, but I didn't like the passageway. It reminded me of a dungeon. It smelled of sewer; green slime was covering the walls, and there was a constant dripping sound. It just gave me the creeps. Another key code later, I was inside the basement of Wu's building. A notification sounded in the building that the vault door had been opened. Completely against protocol, the kids came running to greet me, screaming all the way and arms stretched out wide.

"Auntie Em, Auntie Em," they squealed jumping into my arms. It seems my newly acquired nickname was going to stick. They had just recently watched the Wizard of Oz for the first time. I would forever be their Auntie Em now.

Persia entered the room and chided the children for running for the door without knowing who it was.

"But we knew it was Auntie Em, it's always Auntie Em," Cameron said to his mother, Kim nodding in agreement, making her pigtails bounce.

"Your mother's right, I could have been the big bad wolf," I said holding up pretend claws and chasing the children out of the room. Persia laughed as they ran screaming. She wasn't a stern mother. She reminded me very much of Wu's grandfather, Li. She was quiet and strong, only speaking when needing to. She was elegantly beautiful, and I could see why Wu fell for her so quickly. She had kind eyes and a sweet smile, a genuine Okinawan beauty.

In the next room, the kids hid behind the couch Wu was sitting on. I could see the top of Cameron's spiky black hair and the rounded arches of Kim's pigtails.

"You're up early," Wu said to me not looking up from his book.

"So are they," I said then I jumped behind the couch, and they screamed. They took off to find another hiding place but were intercepted by Persia telling them their breakfast was ready. The children kept vampire hours; it just made more sense. Persia and Song ran the antique store now, so instead of finding a daytime babysitter the kids kept nocturnal hours to spend time with their father. I didn't usually come over this early in the night. Persia and Song had just recently gotten home from closing the store. This was typically family time for them. I hated to interrupt but it wasn't quite dark outside yet, and I couldn't stand to be near Bo right now.

I plopped down on the couch next to Wu and inspected the back of the book he was reading. It was a western, of course; Wu and I had very differing tastes. He placed his bookmark and set it aside when Song, his sister-in-law, came into the room and handed him a clipboard.

"You're ready for inventory," she said without acknowledging me. For the longest time, I thought she hated me. She didn't seem to like Bo or Wu much either, though. I guess she didn't really like anybody. I chalked it up to just a grumpy teenager thing. She had recently turned twenty so maybe she would grow out of it. She was very immature for her age. I'd seen her throw childish fits with Persia, stomping her foot and whining in their native language. She wasn't at all like her sister.

Persia was more like a mother to Song, stern yet loving. Their mother had died when they were still quite young. Persia, being twelve years older than Song, had taken on the mother role as their father was away a lot. I guess it caused Persia to mature quickly, having that much responsibility at such a young age.

Both women were beautiful, with long black hair and almond-shaped eyes. Song had a rounder face, and her hair was just a shade lighter than her sister's was. The big difference was in their attitude and demeanor. How could two sisters act so differently?

"Care to help me later?" Wu asked, breaking me from my thoughts.

I nodded. I don't know why he asked, I always helped him with inventory.

"Are you alright?" he asked.

I just nodded again. I knew I could confide in Wu, but I didn't fully understand what happened this morning, so I didn't want to talk about it just yet.

I hung out at Wu's house until after dark and Bo came over. He didn't like leaving the house before dark, even using the underground passage.

"Ready to go?" he asked, eyeing me cautiously trying to gauge my mood. Bo and I usually went out hunting every night, but I didn't want to go with him today. I couldn't shake the repulsive feeling toward him that my dream left.

"Why don't you two go, I'll go later," I said.

Wu raised an eyebrow. He was used to seeing Bo and I fight. Bo was a stubborn, insensitive jerk most of the time, and Wu had seen us yell at each other on more than a few occasions.

"We need to talk about this, Em, that wasn't normal," Bo said fully entering the room and sitting down across from Wu and I.

"Wait, what's not normal?" Wu asked, concerned.

"She says she had a nightmare, she was screaming."

"A nightmare?" Wu asked with even more concern. "That is odd. I've never heard of a vampire dreaming before. What was it about, what did you see?"

"I don't want to talk about it," I said standing up.

"There's someone at the door," Song loudly interrupted, but I was glad of it. I knew Bo would try to get me to talk if I stayed in the room, so I followed Wu out to see who was at the door.

It was Menelik. Wu buzzed him in. I'd never met the guy, but I knew of him. He acquired documents for all the local vamps. It was him who had gotten Brian and me our passports when we first went to see Angelus. He was very attractive, short brown hair and a square jaw. He was wearing a dark blue suit and carrying a briefcase. He was the common definition of attractive, a very professional looking alpha male type. I took his entrance as my chance to exit, trying to go unnoticed. He nodded to me as he passed. "Miss Polanski," he greeted. I didn't like being called that; it made me feel old, but it was better than Emina.

I went back to our place and sat down at my inventory desk in the storeroom to write in my journal. I know that's so very junior high, but after learning that my memory capacity was limited, I started keeping a journal. In about a hundred years or so, I wouldn't remember my mortal life.

I wouldn't remember my parents, my Aunt Eileen, or Brian. I didn't want to forget them, so I wrote it all down. I tried to make sense of what was going on; maybe it was a fluke, just a one-time thing. Vampires didn't dream; they just didn't...so why had I? Why was it something so horrible? Moreover, why couldn't I shake the horrible feeling of it? I decided not to worry about it; I would put it behind me and not even think about it. I was going to go visit René and listen to her sing at a new club in town. I was going to dress to kill, not literally of course, and I was going to have a good time and not worry about the things that I couldn't explain.

René and I had kept in contact. She was like the sister I never had. She was still living in my old house, and we spoke frequently. She'd been pursuing her singing career, singing in bars here and there. She was very excited about being hired as a regular at Alör, a chic new club uptown. Tonight was her first night on stage, and I promised her I'd be there. I put on a short tight purple dress and some strappy stiletto sandals. The weather was starting to turn chilly, but I didn't care. "Dress up when you're feeling down," Aunt Eileen would tell me when I was younger. I needed to remember to add that quote to my journal. Aunt Eileen had a saying for everything, and it would take me the next hundred years to remember them all and write them down.

I decided to walk to the club. I had a little extra time to kill before René took the stage, and I thought the cool autumn air would clear my head. A group of random hooligans hollered at me, but I didn't pay them any mind. I knew I looked amazing tonight, but I also knew I could easily rip their throats out if they came anywhere near me. After a few unanswered 'Hey baby, where you going' comments they went back to what they were doing, lucky for them. The club had only been open a few weeks, so there was quite a line at the door. René had put my name on the VIP list, so I would get in no problem.

The inside of the club was very nice. It wasn't your regular dance club. It looked more like a high-class strip joint actually. There were long leather couches along the walls; mirrors everywhere and girls dancing behind silhouette screens. The whole place was lit up with blue, purple, and pink lights except the bar that was lit up in green. I'm pretty sure this place was owned and decorated by the Powder Puff girls. I snickered to myself as I went looking for a table. I didn't want to sit on the long couches; they seemed to be the questionable morals section.

I was glad I dressed up; everyone here was dressed to the nines. Was I still in east Tennessee or Beverly Hills? The place was filled with men in suits and girls in tiny expensive dresses. I waded through them and found a vacant table and sat down.

A skinny blonde waitress walked over in a white corset and long black skirt with a split in the side up to her hip and laid her hand on my shoulder.

"What can I get you, darlin'?"

I felt a jolt. She was naked. Wait, she just had on clothes. What was happening? The club was empty now. All the people disappeared. She was naked and having sex with a man in the club; It's her boss. Wait, how do I know that? I shouldn't be seeing this. I shouldn't be here. She's having sex with him to get this job. I don't know how I know, I just know. I shook my head; I didn't want to see this. What's going on?

"Ma'am," she said. "Are you okay?" Her clothes were back on, and the club was full of people again. She knocked on the table in front of me, waving her hand in my face.

"What just happened?" I asked, more to myself than her.

"You were totally spaced out; do I need to call you a cab?"

"No, no, I'm fine. Nothing to drink, thanks."

It happened again, just like with Bo, but I was awake this time. What was wrong with me?

Susan Stumpf

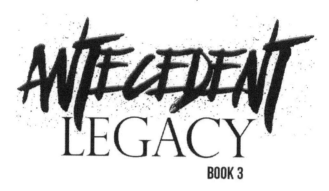

BOOK 3

What if you could see into someone's past and see the horrible things they have done? Could you live with those people, could you still love them?

Em struggles with the emergence of a gift that she doesn't understand and cannot control. Her relationships suffer as she tries to get a handle on it, but can she before someone tries to kill her because of it?

Susan Stumpf is a multi-genre, independent author who brings a realistic gravity to her stories. Her characters are relatable and wonderfully flawed, like herself. She is an Air Force veteran and West Virginia native. Her writing is fueled by copious amounts of coffee and an over active imagination that has prevented her from ever watching scary movies alone. In between novels, you'll find her working with her husband and two children on their farm in southern West Virginia. When she's not chasing kids or shoveling manure, she enjoys movies, reading, hiking, camping, and kayaking.

Find her author page on Facebook.

Made in the USA
Charleston, SC
01 December 2016